PULL YOURSELF TOGETHER

Also by Thomas Glavinic:

The Camera Killer
Night Work
Carl Haffner's Love of the Draw

PULL
YOURSELF
TOGETHER

THOMAS GLAVINIC

TRANSLATED BY

JOHN BROWNJOHN

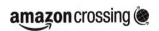

Text copyright © 2010 by Deutscher Taschenbuch Verlag GmbH & Co. KG
English translation copyright © 2012 by John Brownjohn

Pull Yourself Together was first published in 2010 by Deutscher Taschenbuch Verlag GmbH & Co. KG, München as *Wie man lebensoll (How to Live)*. Translated from German by John Brownjohn. First published in English by AmazonCrossing in 2012.

Published by AmazonCrossing
P.O. Box 400818
Las Vegas, NV 89140

ISBN-13: 9781612184326
ISBN-10: 1612184324
Library of Congress Control Number: 2012910421

Those who do not love me may not judge me.

—Johann Wolfgang von Goethe

The night *Challenger* explodes over Cape Canaveral, you're in bed with a girl for the very first time. Unaware of this disaster, you're intent on touching her; decency says you shouldn't. A cassette player is playing music you know the girl likes, so the object of your desire is in the same mood as yourself, impossible as it seems to you.

On touching the female breast you discover that it feels like a sponge for cleaning blackboards.

"Oops, sorry," you mumble.

Claudia says nothing.

Indecent magazines corrupt young people and drive hordes of them into the arms of psychoanalysts. Contrary to what they say, under certain circumstances girls like having their sexual organs pawed, however much the church and the bearded school doctor, whose breath smells of apricot brandy, try to persuade you otherwise. Curiosity and human nature are stronger than the whole bunch of them, God be praised.

You shut your eyes and savor Claudia's aroma. She smells flowery. So fresh and unfamiliar. The smell of another human at such close quarters is a wonderful experience. You can hardly believe that happiness is suddenly pursuing you. When your name is Karl Kolostrum and you've always been the fattest boy in class, you're pretty well inured to nicknames and bullying and far from spoiled where affairs of the heart are concerned. You're lying in an uncomfortable position, but you don't dare withdraw your cramped arm. You're scared any movement may startle Claudia to such an extent that she changes her mind and makes a headlong dash for the door. It's worth the risk, though, so you apply your lips to hers, taking care not to rush things. When mouth finally meets mouth, you're amazed at the sensation produced by such intimacy.

Cautiously, you thrust your tongue into Claudia's mouth without allowing yourself to be distracted by the pounding of your heart. You're at pains to avoid a dental collision. You've read in *The First Time* that this detracts from the romance of the moment and can only be gotten over by laughing it off. But that presupposes a certain degree of preexisting intimacy, and you haven't been together that long. What are three weeks, after all?

You're also careful to avoid salivating into your beloved's mouth. Not to an undue extent, at least. A little saliva is conducive to intimacy, but *dosis venenum facit.*

Your kisses are lingering and ardent.

At regular intervals, Mom uses her plaster-encased arm—a result of alcoholic excess—to hammer on the locked door in hopes of giving you no time to impregnate your girlfriend. Before Claudia's arrival she stated in all seriousness that, because you're still a minor, she'd have to fork out the child support herself. You're to leave your stallion in the stable, as she put it.

You don't react. In Claudia's presence you treat your mother with supercool nonchalance. This will give your girlfriend the feeling that she's chosen a mate who's not only mature but agreeably different from the overgrown kids in her class, with their macho chalk throwing and horsing around. It's 1986, and the same Simon and Garfunkel tape has been playing for the sixth time. You secretly itch to cut the cassette player's cable, but you devote yourself to a preliminary exploration of the female anatomy.

NOTE TO SELF: If your caressing hand slips off and inadvertently lands between the girl's legs, panic is inappropriate.

Claudia doesn't react. Behaves as if nothing has happened. She isn't startled and makes no move to protest, far less take to her heels.

You put your hand between her legs again. And again. For beyond the zipper of her stonewashed jeans lies life's greatest mystery—apart, perhaps, from death. Although you've no idea what sex is all about, you want it. Claudia doesn't. Too bad. At least, not yet. It isn't a question of years, but of weeks. You don't know that, though, because you're only just sixteen.

When the radio alarm goes off at six a.m., you instantly sit bolt upright in bed and utter a yelp because you're immensely jumpy by nature.

As soon as you've calmed down, you think of Claudia. You lie there for another five minutes. Mom knocks on the door and yells at you for being a slug. You're tempted to retort that it's no wonder *she* finds it easy to get up, considering the number of pep pills she stirs into her breakfast coffee. For the sake of peace, you refrain from pointing this out.

"Charlie, time you got up!"

You used to dislike taking showers. The sight of your flabby hips isn't very appealing, and besides, you're lazy. But ever since you and Claudia picked wildflowers and gazed at sunsets together, you get under the shower at every opportunity. You've read in Ovid's *Art of Love* that it's advisable not to afflict your beloved with the nanny goat's mate, meaning the goatish smell of your armpits.

While smearing your person with shower gel, you belt out "Jumping Jack Flash." As usual, you substitute spontaneous interpretations for the original lyrics, which you don't know by heart. You're convinced you've got a nice voice and hit all the right notes, but Mom utters indignant yells and bangs on the bathroom door. You sigh and towel off but are soon humming the tune again.

Because Mom is lazy and fond of hard liquor—a circumstance that, in addition to her penchant for promiscuity, caused Father to walk out on the family—there's nothing on the breakfast table but a smoldering ashtray. She's forgotten to do the shopping again. Or send you to do it for her. Now she absolves herself by calling you too fat and pimply. The less you eat, she says, the better your complexion.

When you're in love, contretemps of this kind, which would normally have led at once to a rancorous early-morning altercation, aren't worth mentioning. Uncomplainingly, you pour hot water over yesterday's coffee filter.

Mom puts a bill on the table the way she does every morning. She doesn't feel like cooking, which is why you've been eating out for months. That wouldn't bother you in itself—Mom's cooking isn't exactly Le Cordon Bleu, after all—but the cuisine of the nearby restaurants does nothing to enhance the reputation of the neighborhood. You stuff the bill in your pocket without a word.

There's still time, so you go back to your room, turn the key, lie down on the bed, and put on your headphones. Usually you listen to hard rock. This morning, however, you drift into one of your favorite daydreams to the accompaniment of John Lennon's "Woman."

You imagine you're muscular, good-looking, and the owner of a motorbike. You ride up to the school on it. Everyone stares at you admiringly. You aren't wearing a helmet, of course, and your forearms are tattooed. Claudia walks over. You take her in your arms and kiss her with everyone looking on. The motorbike is a huge machine like the ones you've seen in road movies. Claudia sits close behind you and you ride in a circle, enviously watched by all the girls in the school.

It isn't until the door bursts open and Mom stands there gesticulating that you realize you've plugged in the headset wrong and deafened everyone in the building. She turns off the stereo system with one decisive move. Keeping an eye on the door, which is hanging off its hinges, you squeeze past her and hurry to catch the bus. Claudia is waiting for you at school.

You fall in love shortly after your sixteenth birthday. Not for the first time, but this is the first time your love has been reciprocated. Therefore, it's your first love.

You stopped being picky after one or two brush-offs. Claudia certainly isn't the class belle. You couldn't even number her among the five prettiest. Truthfully, not many guys would describe her as attractive. And to be absolutely honest, her moon face and large glasses make her look like a fly. But what can you do? Beggars can't be choosers, and since she's a hippie, and nice, and known for her warmhearted nature, you make do with what fate has assigned you.

You meet her outside the school. Apprehensively, you ask if she still loves you.

"Of course I do. You're the love of my life."

"And you're mine."

Ah!

You set off for the classroom hand in hand.

Once there, you hug and kiss Claudia to advertise your secret. You reveal the hickey beneath her ear. It required some effort, like the one on her neck.

This earns you some surprised, half-envious glances from classmates, as well as those bashful smiles that tend to greet sexual activity. Even the American space shuttle disaster recedes into the background. You've no need to be ashamed of the pride you feel. Having a girlfriend means belonging to a victorious caste. It even gives you an advantage over many adults, at least theoretically.

Another thing to consider is that teachers, too, may belong to that sad community of godforsaken individuals who have long led sexually abstinent lives, perhaps because they look like owls or only laugh when they're alone. They can now see how two of those entrusted to their educational care are enjoying pleasures denied to themselves.

As one of a couple you automatically rise in the estimation of others, whether they realize it or not. Who cares if there are more attractive girls in the class—girls with more appealing faces and more alluring breasts? An affair with one of them would cause even more of a sensation, it's true, but the stupid cows wouldn't play ball. Serves them right.

NOTE TO SELF: If you get a chance to enter a relationship you must make the most of it. It's good for your hormones, your experience of life, and your reputation.

You're a member of an eccentric family. At its center are Great-Aunt Kathi and Great-Uncle Johann, known simply as Aunt and Uncle. Aunt Kathi, a lawyer who speaks ultracorrect German, used to be a senior local government officer. Uncle Johann wore the green uniform of the Austrian police. Nobody ever fired a shot at him, though that's not how he acts. He poses as a patriarch, but Aunt Kathi has the last word. No one's supposed to know that Uncle Johann does the ironing and the washing up. Everyone does, though. Women rule the roost in the family.

Everyone quakes before Aunt and Uncle, even Mom. At her office—Mom works as a secretary at an oil company—Mom's greatly feared and speaks her mind to anyone. She's built like a female wrestler and is used to getting her way in all things. At the outdoor swimming pool she enjoys arm wrestling with men. She usually wins too.

There's nothing Mom hasn't tried in her time. For some years, she lived on a farm, where she attempted to hypnotize hens into maximizing their egg output. Since fowl, pigs, and sheep don't lend themselves too readily to hypnosis, she gave up farming and tried collecting jewelry instead. She was so good at it, it'll be 2017 before she pays off her debts on her secretary's salary.

She has preserved her ironclad self-confidence nevertheless. Only to the Aunticles, as Aunt Kathi and Uncle Johann are known (a play upon words typical of Uncle Hans), does even your mother, under any circumstances, never say no.

Although disgusted by her alcoholism, which has gone on for several months now, you're grateful she knows what's going on in the world. She makes no secret of her opinions, so she keeps you up to date on international relations. She's for the nice Israelis and against the smelly Arabs, for the Northern Irish Protestants and against the Roman Catholics, although she isn't quite sure which side the IRA is on. She's also very proud of the foreign expressions she has picked up from somewhere. If you haven't showered for a while, she calls you a *feute*, which is supposed to be French; and if you chicken out of something, you've got no *cochonies*, whatever they are.

Aunt Wilma is Aunt Kathi's sister. She and Uncle Hans are the opposite of the Aunticles: mild, sociable, and easygoing. They're the only rays of light at family get-togethers. You can tell Uncle Hans isn't a blood relation because he cracks jokes and winks at you. He used to bring you the occasional present when you were younger. You like Uncle Hans.

The family consists entirely of aunts and uncles. If it weren't for Mom, you'd feel like a member of the Donald Duck family. Your grandparents are dead; your father sends letters from Sweden with foreign banknotes in them. The whole clan meets once a year, a diabolical spectacle: twelve uncles and great-uncles, sixteen aunts and great-aunts, and you, the sole representative of the generation after them. You've made a list of questions to ask Saint Peter someday, and you plan to raise this point first.

Also present, of course, are family friends the "Bonesetter" and his wife from Tulln. Anyone encountering the Bonesetter for the first time could be forgiven for assuming that he's a war-wounded vet, but his extreme squint is a congenital defect and he owes the loss of three fingers to his lack of skill at handicrafts. You've often had to admire his hobbyist's cellar workshop. He's really an orthopedist and is said to be a quack. According to Uncle Hans, the only certainty is that the Bonesetter isn't very bright because he regards "Bonesetter" as a compliment and has started to use the nickname himself. Although he comes from Tulln, he relocated a long time ago. His practice is in the center of the city.

The nicest member of the family is Great-Great-Aunt Ernestine. You were more or less brought up by her. No one took as much care of you as she did. It was at her place that you watched television when Mom was too poor and the Aunticles too mean to buy a set. With her you ate candy bars and got pocket money and did all the things that were forbidden elsewhere.

Aunt Ernestine lives on the outskirts of town and is regarded as the black sheep of the family. Ever since Aunt Kathi failed in her attempt to have Ernestine certified insane, the two of them have insisted on sitting together at family gatherings. This enables them to exchange icy glares in silence. You're the only one who ever visits Aunt Ernestine. She's ninety-seven years old, extremely thrifty without being miserly, and has a mysterious love of automobiles.

She has retained the robust physique common in the family. If kids fool around outside her house, they can only be new to the neighborhood or young masochists. She comes down on them like a ton of bricks and restores order. People occasionally complain that she has walloped their offspring and threaten to report her to the authorities. When that happens, Aunt Ernestine brandishes her stick and looks so demented that they usually refrain from taking the matter further.

On one occasion the police did show up because of such an incident. Aunt Ernestine went to bed and wept at her neighbors' perfidy. She was a frail old woman, she said, and had never harmed a soul.

"What about the bruises? How did the boy get those?"

"He must have tripped on the way to be interviewed, officer."

There's one other member of the family, Nero. Nero is Mom's seven-year-old Yorkshire terrier, which she bought for some obscure reason from her old friends the Kleibers. She even takes the useless beast to work with her. He's no bigger than a cat and yaps at the drop of a hat. You like the animal, but you're allergic to the smell he gives off. Aside from that, you suspect him of suffering from some mental illness. This is because of various strange predilections for socks and house plants, for instance, but also for vinyl records, which he likes to carry around in his jaws, covering them with slobber and scratches.

If you visit Aunt Ernestine, she gives you money. She's warmhearted, despite being on the eccentric side.

"Just look at you," she says on the doorstep. "You ought to be ashamed of yourself!"

"Why? What do you mean?"

"That haircut! See those boys on the street? How nice they look, whereas you…"

You survey the boys on the street. They've got perms and are trying to grow mustaches. She approves of that.

When someone in authority scolds you for looking slovenly, a diversionary tactic is the only answer. Aunt Ernestine's resentment of the family attained biblical ferocity long ago, so it's enough to make a few remarks about Aunt Kathi's new hairstyle, which you introduce by saying, "Speaking of haircuts..." That ends any further discussion of your own mop. Aunt Ernestine swears like a trooper.

Only then does she welcome you properly. Suddenly, Aunt Ernestine turns mild and merry. She kisses you and calls you her treasure. You're her undisputed favorite. When you visit her you see her face light up. You're happy to see her too—happier than with anyone else in the world. Aside from Claudia, of course.

You have to stand at the window with her. Watching what happens on the street is her favorite occupation. A car drives past. She points it out.

"That's this new Mazda. The Mazda, er, three-twenty. Your mother ought to buy one."

Your response to this advice is a shrug. Mom will never buy a car; she drives too fast and is scared of her own daring. You can't get Aunt Ernestine to understand this, though. You listen for a while to one of the automotive lectures for which she's renowned in the family.

Then it's time to go to the café. She enjoys sitting in the café and getting the proprietors to bring her up to date on current events in the neighborhood.

"But I'm not taking you looking like that! I'd be embarrassed!"

"What's the matter this time?"

"Your hair! Othmar...Wolfgang...Martin...Hans..."—she reels off all the masculine names that occur in the family without hitting on the right one—"go to the bathroom at once and comb your hair!"

It's pointless to argue. Aunt Ernestine is adamant. Besides, at the café you'll get a slice of Malakoff gâteau and a couple hundred schillings. You go to the bathroom and comb your hair and realize you need to take a dump. Definitely, right away, here and now. This is disastrous. Aunt Ernestine is so pathologically thrifty, she refuses to buy any toilet paper. You have to abuse your ass with the daily *Kronen Zeitung*.

NOTE TO SELF: You sing when you're sitting on the toilet. You've always done this.

Because you have a lousy memory, you don't remember the words, so you invent something of your own, something unique and original, and sing it to a tune you know. You've no inhibitions when it comes to spinning out syllables and mutilating words, nor is meaning an absolute necessity. What matters is that the words fit the rhythm. You sometimes forget where you are.

And so, seated on Aunt Ernestine's toilet, you belt out the first words that occur to you to the tune of "Yellow Submarine":

> *In the town where I was born*
> *lives a ma-a-an with a horn.*
> *He is fat and he is mean,*
> *and he's better heard than seen…*

That's as far as you get because Aunt Ernestine is pounding on the door. You're to stop singing in that vulgar manner, she says, and it's rotten music anyway. Aunt Ernestine is the only person who can say such a thing without offending you.

You're in love with Claudia but you still have romantic feelings for her friend Veronica, whose heart you'll never win because you don't possess the requisite looks or charisma (not to mention the courage, character, temperament, luck, sex appeal, charm, patience, or wisdom)—and that's reason enough to indulge in a little *Weltschmerz*.

Besides, you've read in various lifestyle guides whose advice you've long appreciated that self-pity is an emotion you should spurn, but you can still allow yourself a sob or two and a few conspiracy theories because you'll breathe easier afterward.

And it's February, so it starts to get dark in the afternoons. In order to do something daring and impress yourself, which can sometimes have a cathartic effect, you shut yourself up in your room. You're feeling depressed in any case, having just read *The Last Children of Schewenborn* and become even more afraid of nuclear war.

You turn out the light and draw the curtains. You drink black coffee out of a huge mug, even though you find it nauseating without milk and sugar and feel sick to your stomach after a few sips. You smoke filterless cigarettes. Roll-ups would be even more impressive, but you lack the dexterity to make them.

So there you sit, staring into the darkness, which is illumined at regular intervals by the tip of your diabolically strong cigarette, listening to the Led Zeppelin album *Houses of the Holy*. In situations like this, daydreams come about of their own accord.

You're sitting on a bench outside the school, smoking, with a bottle of hard liquor handy. Other pupils pass by, unheeding. You hum to yourself. Being superior to the rest, you don't care what they think. Then along comes Jimmy Page, who's touring Europe on vacation. He sits down on the bench. Unimpressed, you continue to hum. Jimmy is so carried away, he has to sing along with you, like it or not. You converse with your eyes. There's a profound empathy between you. It's a meeting of kindred spirits. Jimmy has to move on, worse luck, but you write down each other's phone number.

NOTE TO SELF: When you're sitting in your darkened room with black coffee and cigarettes, you yearn to meet Jimmy Page.

There's no one around to admire this still life, so you call Harry and ask him to drop in. You need to engage in such maneuvers, unfortunately. You should always preserve an objective image of yourself. When you know you aren't exactly an alpha male, just a universally popular fatty, you have to cloak yourself in mystery from time to time.

Mysterious personalities are never lonely. They need only put out their hand, and along comes someone who's even less suited to being an alpha male.

A little while after you've turned the music down, the doorbell rings. Instantly, you turn the volume up again. The abstracted air with which you answer the door is eloquent with *Weltschmerz*. Tersely, you invite your friend to follow you to your room. Mom has gone barhopping, as luck would have it, so she can't torpedo this get-together.

Fuck!

You forgot to leave some books lying around open—books by authors with resounding names.

"Do me a favor and get yourself a glass. From the kitchen."

Quick as a flash, you discreetly deposit Nietzsche's *Thus Spoke Zarathustra* on the edge of the table, then your visitor comes back in.

Harry asks what happened to the door. You kicked it off its hinges during a fit, you say, but it'll be repaired next week.

"During a fit? What kind of fit?"

You'd rather not talk about it, you mumble.

The glass is unnecessary now. What's the point of a glass when you're drinking coffee? You act distracted, like all gifted individuals are said to be. You get some extrastrong coffee from the kitchen. You also offer Harry a cigarette. It'll probably be too much for him, but he doesn't dare refuse.

You can't think how to begin the conversation. For one thing, you have to act like you're under the influence of pills, as any sensitive person would be. For another, this isn't a child's birthday to be celebrated with good humor and idle chitchat, but a meeting between two persons already on the threshold of late adolescence.

Aware that he's on thin ice, Harry eventually pokes your knee and timidly inquires, at the top of his voice, if the room isn't too dark. It's hard to tell where the other person is, he says, and the music's loud enough to split your skull. Couldn't we turn it down and have a little light? The music and the coffee and the cigarette are great—he's only coughing because he has a cold.

Making it clear that, as host, you're duty-bound to comply with your visitor's wishes even though they don't match your own, you turn on the table light—which illuminates *Zarathustra*.

Further conversation is unimportant. It can only weaken the existing impression, especially if you open your mouth.

"Maybe you'd better split. Sorry I asked you to come."

"What's the matter, Charlie?"

"Nothing. I took three Fincis."

"What are Fincis?"

"Tranquilizers. I was a bit hopped up."

Harry rubs his chin admiringly. You stare at him glassy-eyed. You wonder whether to dribble but decide against it. It might look over the top.

"You mean you're feeling sleepy?"

"I wish. I took two Uzis after that."

"Uzis? Aren't they machine guns?"

He's called you out. Darn it, you knew the word existed. Still, a talent for improvisation can rescue any situation.

"Uppers. They're called that because they work like a machine gun. *Rat-a-tat-a-tat*. That's what it sounds like in your head."

"Oh, I see. Why did you take them, though?"

"I needed to."

NOTE TO SELF: When you're capable of any stupidity, legends come into being.

As soon as Harry has gone, you pour out the frightful coffee and help yourself to some apple juice. The ashtray is emptied, the window opened. The music, which is driving you insane, is turned off. Now that you're feeling awfully lonely, you're allowed to treat yourself to a candy bar, although you're already a good twenty pounds overweight.

You watch television with all the lights on but you're careful to go to bed early enough to avoid a confrontation with Mom when she comes home drunk. There's nothing to eat but French fries and candies and pastries and ice cream. You put off eating until tomorrow.

"**I** just don't believe it," says Paul.

"That makes two of us."

Mom being "sick," you've had to take Nero outside. The woman next door owns a kitten that's slinking across the yard. Ever since he sighted it, Nero has been crazed. He chases the kitten around but is far from intent on biting her. He maneuvers her into the appropriate position with his forepaws and then tries to rape her. She has already cuffed him a couple of times, but he keeps trying.

You're sitting outside the house with Paul, watching.

"Hasn't he been neutered?" Paul asks.

"I don't know. I guess so."

"So what's he up to?"

"I'm not sure."

You haul Nero off the cat one more time. He acquiesces, but two minutes later he's at it again. It's amusing to observe the dog's anguish, the mixed feelings with which he stalks his victim, raises one paw, and then hurls himself into the fray or moves away once more.

"In a year's time she'll have him for breakfast," says Paul.

"Less than a year."

Rather than let the situation get out of hand, you take the rascal back indoors. Paul departs. In an apologetic tone of voice he says he has to study. He doesn't want to repeat another year. You dismiss him with a nod.

After the would-be rapist has been returned to his place in the kitchen, you cut yourself a slice of bread, open a can of sardines, and sit down in front of the television. You turn the sound down. You're bushed. It's been a tiring day. You make yourself comfortable on the sofa and hope Mom sleeps through till morning. You love and are loved by her, and she's quite bearable when sober, but her binges give you the creeps.

In the middle of the night you wake up. You don't know what woke you. You were having a nightmare about Aunt Ernestine. Startled, you disentangle yourself from the blanket, jump off the sofa, and try to get your bearings.

If noises are coming from Mom's bedroom, it's beneficial to a youngster's spiritual well-being if he's too befuddled with sleep to grasp what's going on in there.

You swallow a mouthful of lemonade. What was the dream about? Aunt Ernestine was sick. She needed help.

With both hands extended, you grope your way along the dark passage. You listen at the bedroom door. Mom has a visitor.

Still half-asleep, you return to the living room. What was Aunt Ernestine's trouble?

At just seventeen, you don't hang around, so three minutes later you're on your moped and on the way to her. Your stomach turns over at the thought that something may have happened to her. She's ninety-seven. She's bound to die sometime, but you hope it won't be any time soon. Not now, not tonight.

The cold night air gradually clears your head. When you arrive outside Aunt Ernestine's door, you wonder what time it is. You check your watch.

NOTE TO SELF: When you arrive outside the home of a family member who has telepathically summoned your help at half past two in the morning, you wonder what to do next.

You hesitate to ring the bell because there are no lights on in any of the windows. Then you remember that, family animosities notwithstanding, Mom keeps some spare keys to Aunt Ernestine's home for safety's sake.

You ride home and grab the whole bunch. Mom is still busy. At three a.m. you're back outside the trim little suburban house. You park the moped and unlock the front door.

Infinitely quietly, infinitely slowly, you open the door to Aunt Ernestine's apartment. It's pitch-dark. You tiptoe in. The old floorboards creak, so you lie down on your stomach to spread the weight and you crawl like an Apache. It's ten minutes before you come to a stop beside Aunt Ernestine's bed. The bedroom smells of her. A smell of old woman, of eau de cologne and clean linen.

You can't hear a thing. You panic. Is she dead? She mustn't be dead! Tears flood your eyes. You're in despair. Added to that, there's the spooky awareness of being alone in the room with a dead body.

And then Aunt Ernestine starts snoring. With gusto. The room resounds with a throaty whistle that makes the mirror on her wardrobe door vibrate. You clench your fists, so relieved you can't move. Once you've regained your composure you beat a retreat.

Back home, just as you're replacing the bunch of keys, Mom's bedroom door opens. You dart into your room. You hear her bid her visitor a husky farewell. On the way back to her bedroom she comes into painful contact with the doorjamb.

"Asshole," she says thickly.

NOTE TO SELF: If you're superstitious, it's immensely reassuring to obey your inner voices.

Political arguments are frequent in school. You keep out of them. You've read in *How to Make Friends* that ill-considered remarks can very easily get you in trouble with one side or the other. Given that you lack good looks, talent, and other outstanding qualities, you wriggle off the hook by cracking jokes and being generally disarming, as recommended by the lifestyle guide.

"You attend this school because you don't want to be unskilled laborers," says the history teacher, genially. "What are your professional ambitions?"

"Teaching," you say when it's your turn.

"Teaching, eh? May one know why?"

"Because of the excellent example I'm set here, sir."

Since the history teacher is not genial but a political activist and extremely argumentative, he seldom refrains from probing to see which side you take on one issue or another. Claudia hurries to your aid on such occasions. Being a feminist who goes around in torn jeans and a jacket studded with peace buttons, she embroils him in discussions of principle to which teachers of his type are very partial.

Claudia has blossomed in the interim. Her owlish glasses have been exchanged for contact lenses and her braids for a pageboy cut. She now looks like a fly with contact lenses. She participates so fervently in arguments about the rights of the Australian aborigines that you're absolved from the obligation to take part in them yourself. You hold hands with her.

The fact that no sexual intercourse has taken place after six months does not detract from your affection for her, even though continual masturbation into a sock or the sink is becoming tedious. How can you sleep together when both parties are virgins? Condoms pulled on with trembling, slippery fingers are constricting and uncomfortable, and you're so aroused your erections cannot be maintained for long.

You can't afford to try it without a condom, even if the girl has been taking the Pill. Being a well-informed and conscientious young subscriber to *Your Body*, you know the high risk of HIV from unprotected sexual intercourse. At least Claudia has inadvertently jerked you off twice. Despite her subsequent cries of "Ugh!" and "How disgusting!" you found those incidents encouraging.

Firm opinions are essential if you're to claim a special place in the class community.

"Read any Handke?"

"Of course!"

"Pretty tough, huh?"

"If you use your head just to keep the rain off your neck, maybe you'd better enroll at another school."

You keep out of such arguments. You mutter and mumble to yourself. That, too, is a trademark in itself. Everyone needs something that distinguishes him from the rest. If you're leadership material, you must radiate an aura of superiority. If you have the gift of gab, you must use it. If you're good-looking, you don't have any problems anyway. But if you lack all those things, you must try to be nice and funny and cuddlesome. That takes practice, but even a fatty can go far if he starts training early enough. At least, the author of *How to Make Friends* guarantees this.

It annoys you at first when your classmates nickname you Teddy. That is, until you realize you've won a victory. Really unimportant individuals don't have nicknames at all. That, at least, is what the author of *How to Make Friends, Part Two* believes.

He knows something else as well: The Teddy doesn't rebel like other people; he acquires his status by means of passive resistance. If he falls asleep in class or surreptitiously shares a bottle of wine, hats off to him. Still waters run deep, say the others; Teddy's not a teacher's pet, he's one of us. You enjoy benevolent respect, not least for your elegant habit of failing to turn up for class. The fact that Mom's signature is illegible and she has no recollection of you submitting this or that document for her to check renders it improbable that you'll spend entire mornings in school.

So this is how the Teddy makes his way through life: he conforms, but in a way that's noticeable only to those he wants to ingratiate himself with, not those he's scared of. From *How to Get to the Top*.

When you've gotten used to being called Teddy from time to time, classmates you're on bad terms with start calling you "The Bard." Since they're explicitly referring to a comic book character, you're offended.

NOTE TO SELF: Few nicknames last long.

When you're feeling very lonely, you pray.

Of course, prayer is an eccentric activity. Enlightened people don't believe in God, so there's nobody there to listen to the requests for lottery wins or fine weather. When you're twelve or thirteen, however, and your parents wrongly assume that the occupant of your room is still a child, your loneliness can become so intense that you clutch at any available straw. And, since childlike faith is ineradicable, you sometimes pray at that age.

When you're nearly seventeen, on the other hand, praying is a ticklish business. You feel ashamed. You're almost grown-up, after all. Besides, there's always Claudia, who mitigates your loneliness and usually renders such a drastic course of action unnecessary. But Claudia has gone to Tirol for the weekend.

You're feeling lonely and desperate, so you clasp your hands together and say:

"Dear God, please make me happy. Please make people like and respect me. Please make me feel less lonely. Please make Mom drink less. Please make me lose a few pounds. Please make Veronica interested in me. And please make this awful toothache go away."

Since God helps those who help themselves, you take a painkiller for the toothache. As soon as it works, you call Paul. He's too busy. You try Harry and Philipp. They're both unavailable. You can't think of anyone else. You try Paul again. He now pretends not to be there.

So you lie down on the bed and shed a few tears.

The next day, you visit the Aunticles with Mom, who's sober for once. To celebrate Aunt Kathi's birthday, you're attired like a Confirmation candidate and feeling thoroughly ill at ease, and not just because a nuclear power station has just blown up in the Soviet Union. Anticipating protests from the Aunticles, Mom has banished her jeans, leather jacket, hippie necklace, and other flourishes. She has also insisted that you wear your nice corduroy slacks, your nice oxfords, and your nice new loden jacket, in addition to getting your hair cut. Since you can't afford to incur the Aunticles' thunderous displeasure—even Mom trembles at it— you toe the line. You even have to polish the glasses you've recently started to wear. Mom thoroughly disapproves of their appearance, but you outwitted her by going to the optician on your own.

NOTE TO SELF: If you're overweight and need an aid to your eyesight, you should at least opt for a pair of John Lennon glasses.

You endure the birthday party, to which Aunt Ernestine is not invited, in silence. You find it particularly humiliating to have to join the others at the table wearing carpet slippers (supplied by the Aunticles), which don't scratch the parquet floor but clash with the rest of your festive outfit. You're alone in disapproving of this stylistic dissonance, unfortunately, but you don't dare refuse. All else apart, it would be foolish to rebel because even a hint of recalcitrance would inevitably result in a reduction of the financial donations that are obligatory at family gatherings. And this would be disastrous at a time when you're currently short of cash for buying cigarettes and LPs and hot meals.

What's more, a freeze on donations is not the only form of pressure available to those in charge of your upbringing. For all these reasons, you make the best of things. You listen to ancient hits and agree that they're a feast for the ears. You join in party games. Sing folk songs. Laugh at old jokes. Listen to advice on school, clothes, haircut, physique, and general deportment.

NOTE TO SELF: *When you're sitting there consumed with hatred, remember that youth and dependence will someday come to an end.*

You're feeling sad. Why were you born at such a stupid time? Why not in 1968? That was an era when it was okay to be fat and experiment with drugs and sleep in cars and drive from concert to concert; an era when there was free love and everyone made out, even fat guys—even schoolkids! In the States, at least. The music was better too. In the States, at least.

A Psychological Study of the History of Rock Music states that young people's taste in music tells you a lot about them. If you've no use for current pop and prefer the music of your parents' generation, for example, it can be assumed that you've equally little use for contemporary society and, ultimately, for yourself. *Personality*, a very special book you saw at Paul's and bought from a bookstore the next day, says something else: It doesn't matter when a person is born. There are always people who are too lazy to throw off the shackles of their prevailing circumstances. They are called wimps.

You've been wondering for some time if you're one of those. Is it significant that you'd sooner put your hand in the fire than dare to defy the Aunticles? Can self-control be unwise? You've read in *How to Make Friends* that silence is the supreme commandment because you've too much to lose if you sound off. On the other hand, *A Psychological Study of the History of Rock Music* states that rebellion is the only defense against stomach ulcers.

NOTE TO SELF: Lifestyle guides sometimes play rock-paper-scissors with one another.

The rites of initiation into adulthood include, in addition to one's first abuse of alcohol, one's first experience of sexual intercourse.

On discussing the matter exhaustively with Claudia, you discover that neither of you has ever had penetrative sex, received a blood transfusion, or been addicted to drugs at any stage, so it's likely that both of you would prove HIV negative. Perhaps you should try it once without a condom. Especially since Claudia is taking the Pill.

After school, you're once again lying naked on the bed beside Claudia. An erection manifests itself. Inserting this immediately is prohibited. According to *Kama Sutra for Beginners*, foreplay and prolonged fondling are prerequisites of sexual fulfillment in the female. A sneaky maneuver such as spontaneous insertion would run counter to this, so you manually prime Claudia until she whispers, "Yes, I want it" in your ear.

You endeavor to bring your love tool into play.

A sixteen-year-old girl's yoni is tight, and the yoni of a tensed-up sixteen-year-old girl is tighter still. A sixteen-year-old boy's lingam is hard, but the lingam of a nervous and frustrated sixteen-year-old boy is not an instrument to be relied on in the long run. However, once it's released from the confinement of a condom and, possibly, looked on with favor by the goddess of love, the miracle occurs: you hit the target and effect penetration.

Disbelief. Intense arousal. Startled expressions. What to do now?

You gently, gently, gently start making coital movements. Every ten or twenty seconds you ask Claudia if you're hurting her. You fail to elicit a definite yes or no, so you're at liberty to go on humping away. In spite of all your magazine-fed knowledge, you're audacious enough to inquire, every now and then, if Claudia has had an orgasm yet.

Those first few minutes inside Claudia are a seismic experience, and you will never forget them. So that's what it feels like, you think. Despite its clumsy execution, the procedure delights you. You're quite unaware that the best is still to come. You behave like a clueless driver who floors the gas pedal in first because he doesn't know how to operate the gearshift. The engine roars, but instead of succumbing to a mechanical problem, it attains an inevitable climax. Although this sensation has long been familiar to you from masturbation (revving in neutral), the sex act renders it something quite incomparable.

Overwhelming joy.

The first time you climax during sexual intercourse, you don't utter a sound, and you turn your face away; there's too great a risk of sounding like an animal being slaughtered. As for the orgasmic facial expression familiar to you from certain movies, it could very seldom be considered intelligent.

After the event you both lie exhausted side by side. The sexual aspect is secondary; you're happy to have made it at last. You can't become much more adult than this. You embrace Claudia. Caress her. Light a cigarette. Love her dearly. Would like other people to know. Discover that Veronica has vanished.

Since the sun is shining particularly brightly on this afternoon in the late fall, you mount your moped. Claudia, still completely bemused, straddles the seat behind you and burns her calf on the exhaust. You head to a café where your classmates usually meet.

You sit at a table outside. Order coffee and savor the moment. Rotate your head like an owl on the lookout for acquaintances passing by. When five or six of your friends are finally sitting at the table, you take no part in the conversation. You hold hands with Claudia, hope that your eyes are shining like hers, and let the others' gazes wash over you.

You don't catch what Claudia is whispering to you, you're immersed in a daydream. Muscular and long-haired, you ride up to the school on a motorbike. All your classmates stare at you. They all know that you've had sex—that you're a man. The next moment you're standing on a stage, giving a concert in front of the whole school. You're singing "Woman" for Claudia, who's sitting in the front row. You go over and sing to her. All the female members of the audience are envious. Thunderous applause ensues. You kiss Claudia passionately in front of everyone.

"What's the matter, Charlie? You look like you've swallowed a rat."

You stare at Paul. Hesitantly, you join in the others' laughter. But a moment later you're smiling to yourself again.

You aren't a virgin any longer.

NOTE TO SELF: When you have sex for the first time, you push a door open. The room beyond offers sensations you still can't imagine.

It can't hurt to attend a trial when you're more or less uninvolved—as a witness, say—so it's an extremely interesting matter when Mom, under the influence of barbiturates and peach brandy, hits the next-door neighbor with a poker. Since the victim sustained no serious injuries, there's no danger that your domestic idyll will be disrupted by the imprisonment of a family member.

Even the arrival of the squad car is an adventure. The cops ring the doorbell and ask for the evildoer while cries of pain and outrage ring out in the apartment next door.

"That bitch! That filthy cow! Arrest her, take her away! Here, look, see this blood?"

"Take it easy! Didn't you call a doctor?"

You regard it as your duty to assure the guardians of the law—untruthfully—that Mom isn't home. To admit that she's sleeping it off wrapped in the shower curtain would mean collaborating with the authorities, and rocky though the relations between mother and son may sometimes be, you stand united when confronted by the police. Especially since the woman next door is a cow herself.

You discuss the incident with Mom the next morning. Once again, you're in agreement. You both find her assault on the neighbor edifying. Mom is loath to pay the penalty for it, however. She consults a lawyer on the possible consequences of her mental blackout.

It's decided to plead not guilty. Mom was asleep in bed that night. The neighbor must have sustained her injuries some other way. It's a case of malicious defamation. The principal witness for the defense is—wait for it—you yourself.

When you testify before a court at seventeen, you're so nervous you nearly pee in your pants.

The woman magistrate sympathetically inquires if you'd like an adjournment or a glass of water. To top it all, she addresses you by your first name. It's such an embarrassing performance, Mom and her lawyer start fidgeting in their seats. Fortunately, you end by getting your nerves under control. Not even counsel for the plaintiff's probing questions can shake you.

While you're being questioned, your eyes stray to the left. Two young women are sitting there. They're checking something in a fat tome and making notes, so you assume they're trainee lawyers. They're wearing short skirts and black stockings. You answer the magistrate's questions in an abstracted manner.

Mom's acquittal is followed by an impromptu celebration with her lawyer at the Café Braun. You're continually patted on the back and plied with sparkling wine, but your thoughts are elsewhere.

NOTE TO SELF: When you give evidence in court, you may notice the presence of a lot of pretty women with nice legs.

———— - ————

Once unleashed, a young person's sexuality becomes sheer frenzy.

After school, you have a meal at the Gasthaus Zum Kelch. Then you ride over to see Claudia, who's alone in the house. Swiftly, you both strip and embark on the game of love. It's the same every afternoon, every evening, every night. A fascinating contrast to the old days, when you were still jerking off three times a day and, because you didn't know where to dispose of the stuff, ejaculating into a dirty sock.

When your girlfriend celebrates her seventeenth birthday, she's so disinhibited by drink that, in the course of your pleasurable exertions in bed, she introduces a spontaneous innovation of her own. Lying there stiff as a board, you watch, goggle-eyed, as your *membrum virile* disappears between a pair of lips.

This is an inordinately exciting spectacle.

Quickly overwhelmed by the sensations that accompany this act, you make the mistake of failing to warn your girlfriend that an explosion is imminent. This gives rise to spluttering accusations that you're a filthy beast. You manage to effect a reconciliation

36

with loving solicitude, pleas for forgiveness, and an assurance that this was a unique mishap.

She isn't quick to try it again, but you can wait.

When you get home that evening, it occurs to you to check something that has been exercising your mind for a long time.

Not that Claudia has complained. You've asked her about it, but she shrugged her shoulders and said that everything was fine.

You leave your room to go and get a ruler, then lock yourself in again and think it over.

For a long time you thought you were normal. You didn't beat your brains about it, but squinting left or right in a public urinal gives you food for thought. It could be like driving through town: you keep beefing about the red lights and don't notice the green ones at all. You can't be sure, though. The only answer is to check.

You manufacture an erection, a procedure in which you've had years of practice. As soon as the desired result is achieved, you apply the ruler. Not to the underside of your member but on top, with the end against your belly.

You arrive at an absurd result (five and a half inches can't be right), so the quality of the erection must definitely be to blame. You improve it with the aid of some breathtaking sexual fantasies you'd rather not confide in anyone. You squeeze and stretch and tug away. When you feel you're ready, you measure yourself again. Having now wrung the proud figure of six and a half inches from the ruler, you're satisfied. For interest's sake you measure the circumference as well. This, too, registers six and a half inches. You don't know if that's a little or a lot. The relevant magazines always concentrate on length, and the current issue of *Your Body*, which deals exhaustively with the subject, proves uninformative.

NOTE TO SELF: If you never see anything but red lights in public urinals, measure yourself by all means.

You enjoy hours of tranquility when you visit Aunt Ernestine. That is, as long as your hair or clothes aren't the topic of conversation. You leaf through the magazines she subscribes to: *Auto Review* and *Woman in the Mirror*. Aunt Ernestine lies on her greasy sofa and solves crossword puzzles. There's no talking. This is far from unusual. You feel at home with her, and she enjoys having you there. Besides, the gâteau you've brought from the café imposes a gluttonous silence.

At half past seven it's time to go. You bend over Aunt Ernestine and kiss her on the cheek.

"But I haven't given you anything yet."

"No need, Aunt."

"Bring me my purse!"

Members of the generation born before and around 1900 are unique, as you've had an opportunity to ascertain in Aunt Ernestine's case, among others. Whether smokers, drinkers, workers, or representatives of other endangered groups, the survivors are indestructible. Aunt Ernestine is an exceptional natural phenomenon, and one you can't help grinning at. She may be nearly a hundred, but she's as domineering as the rest of the family.

You pull out the drawer. The purse is lying on top. Beneath it is the lingerie you gave her for Christmas. They're still in their original packaging. You hold them up with two fingers.

"Didn't you like them?"

"Yes, no, er…"

She's embarrassed, but she quickly recovers herself.

"What do I want with new knickers? They're wasted on me. Someone else can have them later on."

By "later on" she means when she's dead. You're annoyed.

"What about you? Why can't *you* wear them?"

"Stop it now and hand me that purse! And go and comb your hair. You're an absolute sight as usual!"

Mom's slippers are under the hat rack, but the dog is home. You take Nero out into the yard. The cat is nowhere to be seen, fortunately. It's been snowing. You flap your arms and urge Nero to be quick. Growing bored, you salute, mark time smartly like a soldier on parade, and sing the tune of the Radetzky March.

What a drag, what a drag, what a dragdragdrag…

You do this with your usual verve until you see a neighbor standing on his balcony tapping his forehead. Affronted, you fall silent.

You open a can of beans. Watch television. The phone rings.

It's Aunt Kathi, wanting a word with Mom. You say she's asleep already. Covering each other vis-à-vis the Aunticles is a long-standing habit in this house.

Aunt Kathi asks you about school. You answer yes and no until she finally hangs up. You help yourself to a Coke. You don't find it worrying that Mom still isn't home.

When shouts ring out on the street at half past ten at night, it's best to act as if you hadn't heard. Not everyone is capable of dealing with the complications that may arise.

According to *Personality*, there are other types of characters aside from the wimp: the trickster, for example, or the conformist, or the adventurer. Only an adventurer would worry about strangers in distress. And there isn't much of the adventurer in you. You did a *Personality* test that proved this. You still haven't dared evaluate it, but you know the answer already.

However, since you suffer from an attribute that romantics term conscience, you steal over to the window after all. There's nothing to be seen, but you can still hear shouting. You make your way downstairs. Although you're scared of getting mixed up in anything, you want to know what's going on.

When you see your own mother running away from two men who are yelling obscenities at her, your heart sinks. You consider going to her assistance. Or ought you to notify the police?

Before you can make up your mind, Mom comes to a halt as if brought up short by an invisible wall. Then she turns around and goes for her pursuers, snarling. The first man she kicks in the crotch so hard, he jackknifes with a scream and collapses. The other guy shrinks away. She attacks him. He retreats, but she's too quick for him. They grapple with each other and roll around on the ground.

When you see your own mother sitting on a man's back, tugging her heavy leather belt out of the loops, then proceeding to thrash him with the buckle, you feel you must be dreaming. The shrill screams emitted by her agonized victim are unworthy of a grown man, and although he deserves a beating, you're glad when Mom terminates this brutal lesson. She jumps up and, swinging the belt around her head, dashes after her other assailant. You watch the two men sprint off down the street, yelling, with your mother at their heels.

You sneak back inside.

NOTE TO SELF: The first time you see your mother involved in a brawl, you decide to join a fitness club as soon as possible.

A ny man who enters into a relationship is saddled with his beloved's family as well.

In view of the disastrous conditions prevailing in your own home, you welcome the attentions of Claudia's beloved Mummy and Daddy. You readily go on Sunday outings with them, listen to family anecdotes over afternoon coffee, and are proud of their invitation to be on a first-name basis with them.

This state of affairs doesn't become a problem until you start to lose interest in your girlfriend. Especially since you continue to cherish Veronica's image in your heart although she is unattainable. Furthermore, one of the more beguiling girls in your class has been sending out favorable signals indicating her readiness for unbridled sex. This shows how your reputation has been enhanced by your affair with Claudia. You may be overweight, but you yourself have become a trophy, and there's no shortage of huntresses!

How to solve the problem? How are you to go to Werner and Anni and say you'd sooner give them back their daughter?

If it were just a question of Claudia alone, you'd cope. You dread the problems ahead but feel confident of being able to overcome them. Claudia will weep. She'll speak of the backpack trips to India and Africa you'd planned to make in two years' time. She'll tearfully point to your joint possessions (a gingerbread heart, a Cat Stevens LP, two torn tickets to a Deep Purple concert, a stuffed toy dog named Maxi) and suggest you both start over.

You'll shed a few tears yourself, of course. The truth is, though, your own enthusiasm for Claudia's hippie talk of love and peace and communes in Goa has cooled perceptibly. As for Africa, you've never given a shit about it. You'll miss Maxi, admittedly. You'll be giving up a whole world with Claudia, but you'll manage. Even if you're sad for a while, because you're always a bit on the sad side.

Claudia's parents are another matter.

You like them. Feel obligated to them. It simply wouldn't do, accepting their friendship and then hurting their daughter's feelings. And the last thing you can tell them is the truth. The only honest thing to say would be: "I'm sorry, but I've got to dump Claudia for the following reason: I'm seventeen years old and itching to stick my prick in other pussies. I know Claudia's like the back of my hand. Claudia's nice and so are you, but I'd like to have sexual intercourse with a different woman each day. I'd even like to go to bed with you, Anni."

You can't be honest for obvious reasons, so what you could say is: "Dear Werner and Anni, I've some sad news for you: Claudia and I have grown apart. We don't see much of a future together, but we're very fond of each other. In time, perhaps we'll manage to reestablish our relationship on a solid footing. After all, what ultimately matters is the road we've already traveled together."

Having often dipped into Aunt Ernestine's magazines, you know how to announce the end of a relationship.

When you've added up your score one afternoon and discovered that, according to *Personality*, you're an 87 percent wimp, you opt for a third alternative: you simply don't show up anymore. You stop going to see Claudia, you don't show your face at her parents' house, you dispense with any explanations, phone calls, or letters. In class you sit beside Paul, and that clinches it.

The most you get, once the dust has settled, is one or two acid remarks from Claudia. But a faint ache persists. A kind of melancholy. The recollection of carefree evenings listening to Led Zeppelin, of a time when you still didn't have a clue.

That feeling is ineradicable.

But you're careful not to mistake it for love. It's akin to nostalgia and homesickness and has nothing to do with your abandoned girlfriend. That's from *Liberal Values*.

You can cope with losing Claudia and not getting Veronica if you temporarily amuse yourself with frivolous Mary, whose pneumatic charms befuddle the senses of numerous guys in their final year—and even of some teachers. Grete, who used to make eyes at you, suddenly wants nothing more to do with you now that you're free of Claudia, heaven knows why.

Mary is no better looking than Claudia. She's freckle-faced and fat, the nanny goat's mate is her frequent companion, and she's certainly not a patch on Veronica. She does have bigger breasts and greater experience, though, and you know from magazines Aunt Ernestine would never subscribe to that an experienced woman is the best thing that can happen to a man.

Not that you're stupid enough to sit next to Mary in class. Everyone knows you're making out with her, and that's good enough. You can't think of anything more beneficial to your image. You're the guy who's on intimate terms with Mary's most intimate places. That's a definite accolade. You may be a fatty, but you aren't languishing on the shelf. Besides, not sitting next to her leaves you free to spread rumors and encourage conjectures. It isn't a grand passion, after all; all the signs are that it's a fascinatingly squalid sexual relationship. So it's quite conceivable that you've also bedded—or are bedding— Sabine, with whom you chat so nicely during intermission. The same goes for Susi. And for Hannah. Charlie's a crafty devil, the others whisper.

You and Mary have retired to the girls' locker room one free afternoon during school sports week and are engaging in sexual intercourse when Veronica walks in, stares at you wide-eyed, and, after closely observing the spectacle for several long moments, walks out again. When that happens, you realize two things: that you'll never stop wishing that Veronica could take Mary's place; and that the embarrassing experience you've just undergone is far from so embarrassing that you wish it hadn't happened. Why? Because it'll enhance the rumors about you. Veronica is not only an absolute dish but given to gossiping.

NOTE TO SELF: *When you fuck, you're a somebody. From* A Psychological Study of the History of Rock Music.

Dancing is a pastime unworthy of the heterosexual male. Nevertheless, there are occasions when you visit the Pravda disco because it's the regular haunt of Iris from the other class, whom you've cast an eye over. In her case, you've wisely picked a girl who also carries a few pounds too many around the hips and suffers from similar skin problems. A guy shouldn't reach for the stars right away. Veronica, of course, is utterly irreproachable. She sits there in class, slim and sylphlike, clean and beautiful, cool and intelligent, a personality unattainable by the fatty in the back row.

NOTE TO SELF: Who you go with is usually a question of opportunity, not volition.

Being in love is always a unique experience. You're in seventh heaven. You daydream. You're a different person. And all this irrespective of whether your love is returned. There are people who deliberately fall in love with the first person that comes along, just to be caressed by this feeling—to reassure themselves that they're alive.

When you're standing at the bar of the Pravda with a group of friends, including Iris, you drink an awful mixture of Coke

THOMAS GLAVINIC

and red wine and play "spoof." Each of you is clutching three coins in his pants pocket. When you take your hand out, nobody knows how many coins are concealed in it. It could be three, two, one, or none. Everyone has to guess the total number of coins in the hands on the counter. The one who comes closest to the correct result drops out and a new game begins. The last to be eliminated buys cocktails all around.

Games like these can be expensive. But if you're lucky and the other players underestimate you, you always drink at their expense.

Girls, including Iris, never play. They cling to their boyfriends' arms and watch. You want to enfold Iris in an embrace.

In the intervals between games you check new arrivals, stick coins in the pinball machine, run your hand over your tight pants, listen to the music, flirt with Iris. These nights out are only moderately amusing as a rule because they resemble most of the nights that preceded them, but if you're in love with Iris you're on tenterhooks. You take note of the guys she speaks with. You reflect on what you and she were talking about earlier. You suspiciously register the glances some dirty dog casts at her.

When you're eighteen and fat and have recently had to start wearing glasses and want to impress a girl, you're inevitably tempted to try to shine at drinking.

And when good music is being played, you stare into space and dream of a brighter future.

You're a rock star returning to the town where you grew up. Everyone competes for your attention. You wear your hair down to your waist and ride onto the stage on a Harley. Your concert is fantastic. Iris and Veronica are standing in the front row, squabbling and wanting to be hauled up onto the stage by the amazing guy at the mic.

You've learned from *Kingpin of the Office in Six Weeks* that smart girls aren't easy meat. You realize you're dealing with a girl of that kind when, after indulging in a rosy daydream in the Pravda, you look around and find she's disappeared.

Total dejection.

You have another drink. The next time the DJ plays a number you like, you stalk onto the dance floor in your leather boots. And that's just what you shouldn't do.

Lit by the rotating mirror ball, you move to the music with narrowed eyes. At a lucid moment you realize you're presenting a cretinous picture and looking the worse for wear. You're clumsy and unable to keep time. Desperately, you try to compensate for your lack of technique by flailing your limbs around more energetically. As in, you bump into other dancers from behind. From the reaction of some friends standing around the floor who are laughing and pointing, you assume you're behaving like a buffoon.

This is the moment when you become aware of how much you'd like to belong, no matter where or to whom. To the nimble dancers, the broad-shouldered bouncers, the popular barmen. To the labor union of the bespectacled, the guild of the ginger-haired, the league of the left-handers. At that moment you sense how alone in the world you are, and how much you'd like to be part of a bigger totality.

It's also the moment when you discover that Iris hasn't gone home but has all this time been hugely amused by a lone dancer's peculiar behavior.

NOTE TO SELF: Sometimes, when you think you've made a fool of yourself, you've really opened a door to something new.

At eighteen your country calls you. Despite her onetime membership in the German Girls' League, the female equivalent of the Hitler Youth, Aunt Kathi is a devotee of pacifism and doesn't want you to do your military service. So it occurs to her that an appropriate medical certificate may spare you eight months in a barracks.

The Bonesetter is taken into the secret. He massages his jaw thoughtfully. "It's not really right," he says, "but I'll give the boy the once-over for friendship's sake. Mind you, it wouldn't hurt him to get a little exercise, and it's rude of him not to have shown his face in my workshop for such a long time."

"What did I tell you?" whispers Aunt Kathi. "You should visit him more often!"

Because you know the Bonesetter of old and have inadvertently smoked some grass shortly beforehand, you pace nervously up and down his waiting room. You're the only patient, too, which seems to confirm the rumor that the Bonesetter is a lousy orthopedist, and prompts you to pass the time by whistling and humming "People Are Strange."

When the receptionist comes in, you fall silent in the belief that your turn has come. But she slinks around the room with an inquiring air as though hunting a mouse. She checks the window, listens to the radiator, opens the door to the stairs, peers right and left. Then, shaking her head, she disappears behind her desk again.

You sit down, pick up a copy of *Bunte*, and immerse yourself in an article about a German princess who's down on her luck. You automatically stop humming when you once more hear the click of the receptionist's clogs. You lay the magazine aside and start to get up, but the woman gestures for you to remain seated.

"Can you hear it too?"

In a sudden fit of persecution mania, you suspect the woman's a spy for the draft board who's carrying out some insidious preliminary tests. So you parry the question:

"I can't hear a thing, I've been a heavy metal fan for years."

"At first I thought it was the gutter, but it only makes those noises when it's been raining. The radiator, maybe?"

She adjusts the thermostat. You're bewildered. You haven't heard any noises at all. Looking mystified, the receptionist returns to her place.

The third time you hear footsteps, you instinctively glance at the radiator, but now the time has come. A moment later you're face-to-face with the squinting Bonesetter. You've never seen him in a white coat before.

"Get undressed and lie down over there," he says, and starts writing something down.

Obediently, you strip to your underpants. Then you hesitate. "Over there," where you're supposed to lie down, there's neither bed nor chair, just bare floor. But because doctors often have peculiar methods of treatment, and orthopedists, in particular, may require exercises to be carried out on the floor, you timidly stretch out amid the skeins of dust drifting across the linoleum.

After a while you hear the scrape of a chair and footsteps. The Bonesetter is pacing up and down, muttering to himself.

"Where are you?" he calls eventually, desperation in his voice.

"Here!"

"Where's here?"

"Here, where you told me to lie down."

You wave. He's staring five yards past you.

"You young bugger," he bellows, "are you trying to make a monkey out of me? You're supposed to lie down on that couch over there!"

Discovering that the words "that couch over there!" are accompanied by an outstretched forefinger, you feel entirely guiltless. There really is a couch over there, but five yards in the *opposite* direction.

The Bonesetter is an intolerant individual, so all your protestations are in vain. You're thrown out. His imprecations accompany you down the stairs and onto the street. You can still hear him shouting from the window six buildings away. "Your impudence will have serious consequences," he yells.

NOTE TO SELF: Christ was innocent too, and they crucified him.

For high school pupils, the weeks devoted to their final examinations are an inevitability.

The outside pressure is considerable. Aunt Ernestine talks of nothing else. It's all you can do to distract her by asking, for the umpteenth time, what her favorite automobile is, and patiently listening to her cockeyed lectures on fuel injection and sports car exhausts. Aunt Kathi calls and urges you to study hard. In the background, Uncle Johann's booming voice declares that getting your high school diploma is a duty to your poor mother. Fortunately, your poor mother's current condition renders her incapable of devoting close attention to the subject of high school diplomas.

You're also infected by the nervousness rife in class. Fellow pupils who usually greet the prospect of any exam with non-chalant derision surreptitiously inquire if you've boned up on your math. You start to wonder if you aren't, after all, con-fronted by something crucial. Being weak at math, you find it hard to remain calm. Only when you obtain permission to sit next to Peter during the exam—Peter, the girls' heartthrob and the best mathematician in the class—do you smoke your intermission cigarette on the school john with the air of a man whom nothing can frighten.

Before the math test you drink several glasses of red wine in the establishment where you customarily eat lunch. This is to arm yourself mentally and show fellow pupils and teachers alike what a helluva guy you are.

When it comes to the exam itself, a cunning plan is put into effect.

The teacher always hands out two different sets of questions, Group A and Group B. Pupils seated next to each other are given different sets to prevent cheating, but because Peter is crafty and quick-witted, and you yourself are too chicken, he takes advantage of the teacher's momentary inattention to switch papers with the pupil diagonally to the rear. The advantage of this is that both rows can copy off each other with ease. Since Peter's handwriting is eminently legible, you pass the math test with distinction.

You've now completed all your written and oral examinations. When the chairman of the examination board utters the magic word "Satisfactory," you experience a feeling of happiness beyond compare. Only now do you notice how important that diploma was, what a weight has fallen from your shoulders, and what a horrific ordeal is now behind you. You've won. You're at liberty to do whatever you want.

One day later, you learn that your objection to the draft board's decision has been sustained, and that, thanks to your severe obesity and an aunt with connections, you needn't become a soldier after all.

You're happy twice over. You put some music on, flop down on the bed, and start daydreaming.

At university, a madman forces his way into a lecture hall and takes the occupants hostage. Veronica is among them. You overpower the hostage-taker and beat him to a pulp, urged on by the others. A grateful Veronica hurls herself into your arms.

The end-of-school festivities flow over you like a dream. Sentimental speeches are delivered, tables danced on. You refrain from the latter activity because you recently broke the two-hundred-pound barrier for the first time. The bullies of bygone years mutate into bosom pals—indeed, into human beings. Conscious of your own maturity, you accept their peace offers. Contrary to a previous agreement, the principal doesn't get a wagonload of manure tipped onto his doorstep after all.

It would be a good opportunity to have sex with some girl or other in the nearby park. In view of your liaison with Iris, you don't take advantage of this. With a trace of regret, you watch couples who have spontaneously hooked up discreetly sneak off and reappear.

When you're drunk enough, you snatch a microphone from someone's hand and belt out a dynamic version of "My Way," for which the audience thanks you with tears and a standing ovation. Everyone squirms with emotion.

You complete your school career with only the most elementary grasp of the most-often-taught subjects and a very modest general education. On the other hand, you've already had sex with three different girls and you've made no mortal enemies.

NOTE TO SELF: That's the most one can expect from one's school days.

When you take your high school diploma home to show Mom, you act as if the piece of paper is nothing special. The truth is, your heart is pounding. You scan Mom's face while she's examining it.

Her eyes light up and you're clasped to her bosom. You give an embarrassed laugh. Contrary to expectations, she makes no reference to the huge new pustule on your forehead. You're floating on cloud nine for hours afterward.

With the high school diploma in your pocket, you lose sight of Veronica. You do, however, manage to persuade your relations to finance (a) a driver's license and (b) four walls of your own. A little flattery, diplomacy, and cajolery, and—for the first time ever—you get your hands on the key to an apartment to which no one else has access. Aside, of course, from Iris, who moves in with you right away.

Aunt Ernestine is the first person you invite to your new abode. You borrow Uncle Johann's old Fiat and pick her up. On the way she complains of the car's inferior quality and complains about Uncle Johann being a skinflint. Driving around in such a rattletrap is undignified, she says. She displays some remarkably detailed knowledge about the manufacture of the Mirafiori. You listen to her with only half an ear.

The centenarian marches through your apartment like a sergeant major. Everything is inspected: the antique bedside table (nice!), the kitchen (no ventilator hood?), the bedroom (hmm), the mattress on the floor (well, really!). Then comes coffee. Aunt Ernestine stirs her cup and gazes into space.

"So this is how young people build their nests," she says.

There seem to be stereotypes in every person's life, especially when it comes to love. For whatever obscure reason, some women fall for men who beat up on them; others keep getting involved with younger men. Some men have a preference for overweight blondes; others fall prey to disastrous obsessions and become infatuated with their stepmothers, their sisters, or their female bosses.

Once you have your high school diploma behind you, you discover you also belong to such a group.

Iris has an Italian cousin you'd far rather be with than with Iris herself. Cousin Paoletta is even more unapproachable than Veronica. She's several years older than you, will soon be majoring in archaeology, lives on her own, and has a long, slender neck with an amber necklace dangling from it.

You'd never dream of trying to make a pass at her. The very thought of such an approach would be blasphemous. It would be like a fat, arthritic dachshund making advances toward a Dalmatian. But on the fairly frequent occasions when you go out with Paoletta and Iris at night, you could weep with frustration.

NOTE TO SELF: When you spend a lot of time socializing with a woman you really lust after—when you go walking and swimming with her and are unmistakably shown what you'll never possess— you feel as sick as a dog.

Discounting such adverse circumstances, these first few weeks of freedom are wonderful. When you've passed your finals you feel you're on top of the world. There's absolutely no reason to make grandiose plans for the future. It's enough to lie in bed under the influence of cannabis and listen to psychedelic music. You've never been happier. All the pressure has gone. Everything's fine.

You only occasionally emerge from this pleasurable condition. Preferably, when the dope has run out.

"Charlie," calls Iris, "do you realize you sing to yourself the whole time?"

"Me? Sing? Surely not?"

"The whole time, Charlie. You kind of yowl and whimper, and so softly, it sounds like a cat shut up in a closet."

O n the days when Iris has to leave the apartment early because she's gotten it into her head to do an internship at the local radio station, you fish the newspaper off the doormat and make yourself a lavish breakfast. Between the third roll with jelly and the ham on toast, you go downstairs to get the mail.

Envelopes suspected of containing bills you don't open; you shelve them till later or the next day. Although you seldom receive anything else, you're absolutely obsessed with the mail. You can't shake off the feeling that something great may come your way by post.

After breakfast you take up your position at the window and say good morning to the old lady across the way, who spends the mornings gazing out her own window. You look down onto the street and cogitate.

Involuntarily, you wonder what to do with your new life. You don't want to be a teacher anymore. Being a teacher means shaking hands with the devil. There's nothing to do but go back to school, because the alternative is called work. But to study what? And what prospects are introduced or cut off by the decision you make?

It's not as if you don't have any interests. What you'd like best would be something to do with music. You enjoy singing, and thanks to Aunt Ernestine's numerically impressive record collection, you appreciate music. You'd like to sing with a band, but you don't have the guts. Or the talent either, probably. You'd like to go on tour with bands. As a roadie, a sound technician, or something. But you don't know anyone in the business.

For want of anything else to do, you go to the students' advisory service.

"What are you interested in?" inquires a sophomore with a goatee and steel-rimmed glasses.

"Women," you answer.

He laughs. "Aren't we all? I mean, where do your talents lie?"

"I can sing."

"Why not try the music academy?"

"Hmm, better not."

The advisor doodles circles on a piece of paper with a smudgy ballpoint. Outside you can hear the clatter of trays in the students' canteen, a babble of voices, the clink of bottles.

"Don't you have any interests at all?"

"I wouldn't put it like that."

The circles on the sheet of paper slowly, infinitely slowly, evolve into a snail shell. The advisor rolls himself a cigarette. Shyly, you avoid his eye.

"In your case, only one thing occurs to me," he says at length. "Art history. It has the best-looking girls. But don't blame me if nothing comes of it."

You study art history. Like you, the guy in the steel-rimmed glasses was telling the truth. There's no other major with lectures attended by as many good-looking girls. And it's a good choice where your reputation is concerned. There's an aura of nobility about anything to do with art. It's a ticket, not only to intellectual circles but to swanky suburban villas. And when you've graduated, you can become a museum director, earn a lot of money, and get to know plenty more beautiful women. It's a sensible decision, hormonally as well as financially. At least, that's what you infer from *Choosing the Right Course*.

Since you've no idea what awaits you, you enjoy being a student. You take an interest in all aspects of student life. Even lining up in the cafeteria becomes an adventure. You're delighted to note that many of the lecturers are on first-name terms with the students.

Being a fat young freshman, you think it advisable to stroll the lanes of the inner city in a black hat, a black cloak, and a white shirt with a stand-up collar. A three-day beard signalizes that you're at ease with yourself and the world in general. You eschew smoking a pipe; it might overdo your image.

So student life brings recognition and presents advantages on several levels. You particularly enjoy the communal visits to bars after lectures. You drink coffee or beer or wine, you get to know people, and you practice the art of exuding charm. You've come to terms with the fact that you're no Adonis, but you sense that there are women who have no rooted objection to corpulence. As long as you're well turned out, and pleasant, and amusing, you'll make out.

By now you've learned what is especially important when mixing with women. Smiling. Being friendly. Paying compliments. Being attentive. Praising a new hairstyle. Noticing a new blouse. According to *Anyone Can Be Nice*, slim and good-looking men don't bother to do that. That's where you come in.

Because Paoletta is out of your league, knowledge of this kind certainly won't help you with her, so you don't even try.

Evenings are the nicest time of day in a student's life. If you manage to borrow some money from somewhere, you meet up with your friends at gastronomic establishments and imbibe spirituous liquors. If the get-togethers take place on private premises, so-called soft drugs may come into play, though these are to be avoided from the sexual standpoint because they have an adverse effect on your libido.

NOTE TO SELF: Pot smokers are no good in bed.

Flying with alcohol and/or marijuana, you sit together and discuss the burning issues of the day. The economics major looks like the epitome of a student with his long braid and Jesus sandals, and you're proud to know him. The education major talks of self-discovery seminars in the woods and raves about his drums and his loincloth. You listen wide-eyed. It certainly takes all sorts to make a world! The female anarchist interrupts the education major by slapping him on the forearm. She calls for more and better beer. You don't care about the beer. The music's good and the girls are pretty, that's what matters.

You notice in the course of these parties how urgent the Iris problem has become. You suffer from scruples, so you don't want to cheat on your girlfriend, but these nocturnal gatherings are so big that even a fatty could pick up something. There's always some lonely girl who'll make do with leftovers at three in the morning, and it's hard being fat and saying no. Especially since you don't know if you're still in love with Iris.

The fact is, you're confronted by the same situation as you were in a couple years ago. You discover that the same problem always seems to crop up: you're in a relationship but would like to have sex with other girls. The nature of a monogamous liaison doesn't permit this. All that remains is cheating, splitting up, or excessive masturbation.

NOTE TO SELF: Human sexual relationships are an ill-developed system displaying grave deficiencies.

At nineteen you're faced for the first time with one of the trickiest problems life has to offer: How do you gauge whether you're still in love with your girlfriend?

———— - ————

When you've passed your prelims at university, you go to see Mom and—casually but with covert pride—show her your grades. She has gotten something of a grip on herself recently. She seldom touches alcohol, and she has given up pills altogether. But she doesn't show much interest in her son's academic progress either. Other than your high school diploma, she merely glances at the rubber-stamped report, says aha, and goes into the room next door to fetch the diet pills she got for you.

"Even my boss passed a remark. He saw you on the street. The next day he came to me and said, 'Your son has been putting on weight with a vengeance.' That's what he said. And you were singing to yourself—'caterwauling,' as he put it."

In addition to some new underpants and two pairs of checked socks, Mom gives you some face cream. She reinforces her wish that you adopt more sensible eating habits by saying that a blotchy complexion comes from snacking on sweet things. You fold up your report and wave Mom a grateful good-bye.

Because you don't pursue your studies with excessive zeal, the time you save presents an opportunity to inform yourself about political and cultural developments. This is important; it hones the intellect and refines the character. You derive the requisite information from a liberal weekly favored by Social Democrat high school teachers.

These months are a time of true political socialization. Although you don't really grasp the significance of the fall of the Berlin Wall, being young and Austrian, the sight of those jubilant crowds brings tears to your eyes. Issuing from countless throats, the cry "We are the people!" impresses you and gives you goose bumps. You rejoice with those people. Secretly, you wish the mob would also massacre the East German politburo, but you keep that to yourself.

At Thursday meetings of the Austrian Socialist Students' Association, you keep out of the debates. You got into it almost by accident, having been taken along by some fellow students, and now you spend every Thursday sitting in the musty-smelling cellar where its meetings take place.

Commonly known as FAUST, or FIST, from its German initials, the Austrian Socialist Students' Association is a worthy and congenial institution because, in addition to fostering political awareness, it helps to familiarize female students from the backwoods with the idea of free love. When the FIST chairman reminds his audience that it's bourgeois to be prudish, you direct a faintly authoritative wink at a plump girl sitting nearby. No shots are ever fired and the group's revolutionary fervor restricts itself to the painting of banners calling for solidarity with Cuba, but—as the chairman says—happy agitprop has to pave the way for every revolution.

You enjoy listening to such speeches and notice what an impression they make on various rustic belles. For the hundredth time, you regret being sexually tied. Although you can't rid yourself of the suspicion that the chairman himself isn't 100 percent convinced by the content of his harangues and is more interested in paving the way for revolution by carnal means, you don't hold it against him. You sit there, pass around "our Joe," as the joint is affectionately known, and delight in being alive. And afterward, when you make love to Iris, you preface penetration with the current definition of German reunification:

"Now grows together what belongs together."

When you've got Mirko's dick in your mouth, you suddenly wonder what you're doing. It doesn't taste nice and isn't sexually arousing. The fact that your own dick is in Mirko's mouth doesn't improve matters. The only surprise worth mentioning is how warm someone else's penis feels.

For reasons of total erotic futility, you discontinue the experiment. Quickly, you down another glass of the *vin ordinaire* that got you into this situation in the first place. When you convey to Mirko that you don't care to repeat the experiment, you're relieved when he replies in the same vein.

But you don't really regret having tried such a thing once—not, anyway, after you've gargled and rinsed your mouth out. At least you now know how women feel during oral sex—or rather, you hope they don't feel the same. What's more, from now on you can claim to have experienced gay sex. In the circles you move in, that doesn't harm your image.

Mirko is a medical student. He's the son of a dentist, not that this prevents him from having bright yellow teeth. A nice guy, he suffers from a compulsion to try everything once. He parachutes from ten thousand feet and takes cooking lessons from his Indian and Chinese neighbors. He races go-karts and bungee-jumps off bridges, patronizes strip clubs, tries drugs. He pursues women, plays cards for money, scuba dives, plays the trumpet, flies kites, was national Hully Gully youth champion, and drinks like a fish. You haven't met a more interesting guy at the university. He says you're too much of a wimp and proposes to take you under his wing. You're convinced that not even he dreamed of the lengths to which that project would take you.

One night, when Iris comes home just before dawn, you grouchily ask her where she's been. You don't listen to her reply, just get into bed and redevote yourself to *Betty Blue*.

"Did you hear what I said? I had sex with another man."

"You did what?"

"I had sex with another man."

Interestingly enough, the first question that occurs to you after she makes this confession is banal in the extreme.

"Who?"

NOTE TO SELF: Any man in this situation asks the same question, whereas women react differently. Their response is "Why?"

So, shortly after your twentieth birthday, your girlfriend cheats on you with a philosophy student in his tenth semester. You have sex with Iris immediately after learning this. Some more unpleasant dialogue ensues.

"Did you at least use a condom?"

"There wasn't time."

"Have you known him long?"

"He's in my introductory seminar."

You're surprised at the cool way in which Iris responds in the affirmative to these and other questions (Did she have oral sex? Did she enjoy it?). She says she wanted to know what it was like to go to bed with someone else. Everything else aside, she says, you're too fat. This candor leads to other awkward questions, for instance about the size and nature of the offending member and its proficiency. When you've tortured yourself sufficiently, you go to pieces. You feel hurt, dishonored, betrayed.

NOTE TO SELF: It's tough being cheated on.

For someone whose libidinous inconstancy has long caused him to consider ditching his girlfriend, it's a shattering experience to be ditched oneself. Quite apart from the sense of outrage, there are practical disadvantages to be dealt with, and if you're an 87 percent wimp, these considerations send you into a panic. Who'll do the cooking? Who'll do the housework? Who'll fix the dental appointments?

A situation like this needs handling with care, but you can't deny it has its positive aspects. You can now participate uninhibitedly in the regular Thursday evening indoctrination sessions for young female socialists without being so conscience-stricken afterward that you can't sleep a wink. You take your dirty laundry to Mom and collect the clean items. You're constantly on the lookout for girls you could go to bed with. You never stop looking, even when you're thinking of something else—even when you're roaming a bookstore in search of a particular title or cursing as you fix a bicycle tire that has yet again failed to withstand the rider's weight. *Your Body* says it's a genetically programmed urge to scatter your seed. Taking a less charitable view of the matter, you could equally call it a genetic defect.

Weary from the brain-softening practice of smoking grass, you wonder if studying art history was the right decision. It's awfully tiring, rising early in the morning and getting to the university in time for some boring eight-thirty lecture. You'd far rather devote yourself to reading novels by Karl May. You lie in bed and read *Winnetou II* or *Satan and Iscariot* for the umpteenth time. Imagining yourself in the Wild West while rain comes pattering down on the windowsill conveys a snug sense of security.

More congenial still than being at home, or even at the university, are afternoons in the Café Schiller, where one can pass the time by playing board games, feeding the pinball machine, reading newspapers, or chatting with people. Artists and other idlers go there during the day, pretty women in the evenings. It's an idyllic place.

You're woken one morning by someone hammering on the door of the apartment. You sit up with a groan. You don't really want to open up, but the hammering is so insistent that you're positively compelled to grope your bleary way to the door and open it.

NOTE TO SELF: When a muscular man with a mustache and wearing a gold chain stands on your doorstep and asks if you're the person you are, you'd prefer not to be that person.

You deem it inadvisable to lie to a man of his appearance, so you nod. He introduces himself as a debt collector for the newspaper you've subscribed to but never paid for. He wants the money on the spot; otherwise, he says, property of the same value will be taken.

The man refuses to accompany you to an ATM. With difficulty, and not without perfidiously smashing Iris's piggy bank, which she inadvertently left behind, you manage to scrape together the outstanding balance. The debt collector mutters a good-bye. He has never once looked at you the whole time. When the door closes behind him, you flop down on the bed and brood.

The first time a debt-collecting agency comes down on you, you resolve to open all the letters you receive, bills included.

Although pleasant, a life of idleness requires financing. Curiously enough, you're shy about asking Aunt Ernestine for money. She would give you some in a minute, but your conscience pricks you. You take whatever she slips you of her own free will, but begging her for money would seem a betrayal. So you try Aunt Kathi.

"I know you give me plenty, but I've got problems."

"What's the matter with you?" asks Aunt Kathi. "More money, always more money! Where will it end?"

Unmoved, you cite the outrageous prices charged for standard works on the history of European art—indispensable learning aids, in other words.

"Then you'll have to find yourself a job."

"I already have a possibility."

"I see. When do you start?"

"The thing is, I have to buy myself a book today. I can't sit this next exam without it. I need the money now. Please, Aunt."

She gives you a five-hundred-schilling bill. In return, you're asked to patch things up with the Bonesetter for one thing, and, for another, to carry a stack of wastepaper downstairs to the recycling bin. You kiss Aunt Kathi on the cheek.

Deep in thought about how long the five-hundred-schilling bill will last, you chuck the bundle of newspapers into the bin. At the last moment, just as you're about to close the lid, you're hit in the eye by a pair of boobs on a magazine cover.

You're simultaneously amused and embarrassed to discover that an elderly uncle of yours browses porn magazines.

Having fished out the magazine with your fingertips, you go home and examine your find. It not only contains personal ads of a suggestive nature but is lavishly adorned with illustrations of various sex acts. It's the kind of thing you pored over at fifteen when Paul came visiting. You never had the guts to buy one yourself. Now you're of an age when it would no longer be illegal to reply to the ads from a "low-down and dirty blow-job artiste" or a "charming filly who likes it both ways."

NOTE TO SELF: Buying raunchy magazines is thoroughly conducive to expanding your knowledge of life.

Looking carefully through the magazine, you come upon a series of ads it might pay to reply to. You compose some replies in your head, jerking off the while. Strangely enough, your enthusiasm for potential pen pals evaporates after you come.

That evening in the café where you've arranged to meet a girl student who, despite her double chin and pasty complexion, has twinkling eyes and dimples, you use an old and proven method. Arriving there before her, you immerse yourself in a book by a celebrated author of towering intellect and put it down on the table, jacket up, when she appears.

NOTE TO SELF: One should never underestimate the effect made by casual, unaffected intellectualism.

Because you're relaxed and at peace with the world that day, you're fortunate that the girl declares herself willing to come back to the apartment with you. Once you get there, however, problems arise. You're unsure if she wants to copulate.

As you lie between her legs and inhale the ascending aroma, you're so aroused you're scared of coming. Nevertheless, you carefully apply your tongue and lips. You lick and suck and nuzzle for five minutes, ten minutes. She writhes and moans. Twenty minutes. Half an hour. You wonder whether your foreplay has attained the prescribed minimum duration.

Many years later you'll realize what was going through your fellow student's mind:

"When is this guy finally going to do something?"

W hen you're twenty there's a general election. This means you can do your civic duty for the first time. Together with some friends, you throw a party to mark the occasion, taking care to even out the sexes. There's nothing worse than all-male get-togethers. According to *Personality*, men are generally less intelligent than women and more socially and communicatively limited. An evening in exclusively male company is like a chimpanzees' tea party. The sexual aspect plays a role as well, of course, but even a mixed party with predominantly ugly women is preferable to an all-male one.

The party in Edith's apartment begins at two a.m. This is because by five, when the first results come in, everyone must be drunk. It's been known since time immemorial that no party can succeed in default of a pathologically excessive consumption of hard liquor.

The majority of those present belong to the Socialist Students' Association, which perceptibly inhibits people's freedom of expression. Not that you intended to express an opinion of any kind.

The party starts running out of steam around four a.m., so it's extremely opportune when your hostess announces she's ripe for sexual intercourse. You retire to a minuscule bedroom with her and have sex.

"What's the matter? Something wrong?"

"When I feel like a fuck," says Edith, "I sit on top."

"Sure. Sorry."

NOTE TO SELF: After sex you always feel you've completed a mission.

Back outside you come across an interesting Young Socialist. She's talking to some guy in a corner. Her face is slightly disfigured by scars, but you fancy her all the same. She isn't as pretty as Paoletta, of course, but since you aren't as good-looking as Aaron, the actor Paoletta currently shares her bed with, you'd be on equal terms.

Sex is said to be a product of opportunity, but that's wrong. It would be truer to say that opportunity *alone* generates sex. Or at least, the kind of sex that provides a little fulfillment. (From *A Psychological Study of the History of Rock Music*, on the subject of Mick Jagger and Jerry Hall.)

As you walk past the girl you hear her say:

"Why on earth did you drag me here? It's a total non-event!"

You'd really meant to speak to her. Now you don't dare.

The election results plunge the apartment in gloom. The conservatives have lost, admittedly, but the extreme right has made big gains. Beers are drunk, arguments deployed.

Being less interested in politics than in primitive filth, you pay another visit to the adjoining room with Edith.

After that, you've experienced all that such parties have to offer in the way of what makes life worth living. Since you're ignored by the scar-faced girl, whom you can't tear your eyes away from all night, you wave to everyone and split. Nobody calls and urges you to stay.

In a situation like that, it's advisable to go home and jerk off, thinking of the Young Socialist.

Later, you feel ashamed. You drink some apple juice and reflect on the subject of men. Men are the pits. All that puzzles you is why it's such fun to be one.

If you're fortunate enough to witness the day when Germany is reunited, you can't help feeling melancholy. Still, at least you've no need to feel so scared of a nuclear war. While watching the celebrations on television, you debate whether to call Iris or Claudia, whom you occasionally meet for coffee.

When getting down to your nightly masturbation, you remember Uncle Johann's magazine. You fish it out from under the bed, look up the most appealing ads, and reply to them, meanwhile masturbating like a madman. Since you know if you wait you'll never mail your replies, you take the envelopes and go out. While inserting them in the mailbox, you feel sure you're the first person who ever stood in front of it with such an agonizing erection.

Now you've done it. Being as lecherous as you are, you can't wait to receive some mail.

You go back to the apartment and can finally jerk off to a finish. Then you go to the bathroom, wash your hands, and slap your face hard. Once, twice, three times.

You've really done it. Having sobered up, you pray you don't get an answer.

You consider blowing up the mailbox with fireworks, but someone who, percentagewise, corresponds so fully to *Personality*'s definition of a wimp isn't the suitable person for such a venture.

NOTE TO SELF: In a state of sexual arousal, one resolutely contemplates doing things that later strike one as curiously unappealing.

When you look in on the Socialist Students' bar later that day, universal dejection is all you encounter. "They should have divided Germany into quarters," says one guy. "I'm prepared to fight," says another.

You get out of there in a hurry.

You go and drink a beer at the Priamus, your regular haunt. You play cards with some Turks, turn your head to inspect every woman that comes in, feel lonely, wish you had a girlfriend, wonder why people make so much of a fuss about politics. It doesn't matter who's in power as long as it's not a dictator. What matters is to feel safe in your own home, spend some enjoyable hours in front of the television, and fall asleep with someone beside you.

If you look for a girlfriend you won't find one. If you do happen to find one, other interesting candidates show up. This is a very important realization, but one that's useless when you're looking for a girlfriend.

That night you decide to visit a brothel for the first time in your life. Your reasons for doing this are only marginally sexual. You've grasped that sexual intercourse is far more than a means to the most enjoyable ejaculation possible. It signifies the most intimate connection between two people that can exist. So you try to discover if that connection can be bought.

You leave the brothel one illusion the poorer. Besides, it dawns on you that you've just blown the price of your evening meals for the next two weeks. Still shaking your head, you buy tomorrow's paper from a newsstand.

You lean against a hydrant and study the job listings. Your eyes widen when you spot a photo of yourself on the personal ads page opposite. Beneath it is the following:

> *Let's drink a toast, hip, hip, hurray,*
> *our Charlie's twenty-one today.*
> *May health and wealth be his forever,*
> *and may good luck desert him never.*
> *Mom, Uncle Johann and Aunt Kathi,*
> *Uncle Hansi and Aunt Wilma, and*
> *the Bonesetters from Tulln!*

When something like that happens to you, you feel you're gazing into the abyss.

At first you wonder if it would be feasible to remove every barroom copy of the paper from circulation. Out of the question. That ad will make the rounds.

You take a closer look at the photo. It's an old snapshot, probably from the Christmas before last, but a flattering one. At least you needn't feel embarrassed about your appearance.

You wonder if Paoletta will see the ad.

It's a strange sensation, knowing that a hundred thousand people are about to learn of your existence. If Mom, the Aunticles, and even the Bonesetters hadn't had a hand in it, you might even take to the idea.

80

You stroll home with the paper rolled up in your hand, daydreaming.

You're a noted art historian being interviewed in a beer garden by a pretty young female journalist. A gang of bikers zooms up with an earsplitting roar. The people around you take off because the gang is notorious for violence and mayhem. The journalist also starts to get up, but you calmly put a hand on her arm. The gang leader says hi and asks how you are in a friendly, respectful tone of voice. You remove your shades and act like you're trying to remember who he is. You're polite in a condescending way. The gang zooms off. Everyone gazes at you admiringly. Paoletta, who is nearby, has witnessed the whole incident. The journalist asks how you manage to wield so much authority over such types. You shrug your shoulders.

When you don't have a girlfriend, don't know what to do with yourself at school, are loath to further your self-education, and can see little prospect of reconciling your self-image with reality, you tag along with Mirko to the Jack Point.

The Jack Point is a huge amusement arcade. Women are hardly ever seen there, unless you count the occasional denim-jacketed fifteen-year-old with a cheap perm, a cigarette dangling from her lips, and a punk boyfriend. The regular clientele consists of youngsters with bad teeth and individuals of indeterminate age whose pebble glasses and downcast gaze are reminiscent of raincoated flashers. The prevailing atmosphere is that of a peep show. Nobody takes any notice of anyone else. Everyone avoids personal contact. Nothing can be heard but the burbling of the slot machines.

If the Jack Point were a place where people did notice each other, you'd soon have become a well-known figure there. A plump young man in a black cloak, white shirt, and black hat is no everyday sight, the more so when he's always singing to himself. Fundamentally, though, you're glad no one gives you a second look. The society you mingle with in this arcade isn't the finest, especially since there's a down-and-outs' hostel around the corner.

The food in the cafeteria is revolting—you can smell old fat and see flies feasting on the pastries in the glass display cabinet—but it sells the best potato salad far and wide. Your conscience pricks you when you gorge yourself on five or six portions in succession, but you can't get enough of the stuff.

NOTE TO SELF: When, on your second or third visit to the arcade, you discover the diabolical five-schilling slot machine, you set off down the primrose path to perdition.

You insert a five-schilling coin. It's shoveled onto a heap of other coins. If you're skillful and in luck, the inserted coin causes the unstable, randomly constructed edifice of fivers to collapse. When that happens, three, four, or maybe even twenty fivers fall into the tray. Then you can pocket them.

The machine is diabolical because, for all your care and putative skill, the fivers that fall into the tray never outnumber the coins you insert. You never acknowledge this. You'll try just one more, you say. You repeat this to yourself until you've lost far more money than Aunt Ernestine is prepared to donate to you per day.

If you want to get rid of this and other forms of frustration, it's advisable to work it off on the pinball machine.

When you change money at the Jack Point, you count it. You give the cashier a hundred-schilling bill and he deftly plunks down two piles of ten five-schilling coins. Or so you think until you check and find there are only nine fivers in each. You start to complain, then drop it.

Minutes later you wonder why you're suddenly feeling so depressed. As if you had to be prepared for a threat of some kind.

You recall what you've read in *Personality*: the wimp doesn't complain when cheated while shopping. Yes, that's what it said, word for word, and you were invited to put a cross in the appropriate box:

☐ Every hour
☐ Every day
☐ Every week
☐ Often
☐ Sometimes
☐ Seldom
☐ Never

If you're a wimp, you don't sit down until every last person in a streetcar is seated. If you've managed to secure a seat, you jump to your feet if an elderly woman gets on, purely to avoid being told off. Every week.

If you're a wimp, you never contradict anyone, even if you don't share their opinion, because you don't want to risk alienating them. Every day.

If you're a wimp, you don't resist when someone pushes in front of you in a store. Often.

If you're a wimp, you tell the plumber everything's just fine even though the faucet's still dripping. You shrug your shoulders and tell yourself you're sparing your nerves. Seldom, but only because your faucet seldom drips.

B ecause Aunt Kathi believes that a young man should forge acquaintanceships with influential people as early in life as possible, and because she additionally regards the Bonesetter as someone with "connections," she insists that you cultivate good relations with him and pay him a visit from time to time.

Nothing can be allowed to stand in the way of Aunt Kathi's wishes, so you one day dial the Bonesetter's phone number and ask how he's getting along.

You're surprised at first to be promptly invited to visit. On mature reflection, however, and after consulting *Identify the Four Character Types*, you understand why. The Bonesetter is a lonely individual—not even his wife listens to him—and forever in search of innocent victims to whom he can recount his life story and show off his workshop. It's been a good two years since you were last down there, and you shudder at the very thought of that cold, smelly cellar.

Gritting your teeth, you set the alarm for seven a.m.

The Bonesetter answers the door. He ignores your opening words and taps the dial of his wristwatch. It's two minutes past eight. You apologize. The bus was gridlocked, you tell him.

He offers you some coffee. You say yes, but he's already on his way downstairs and beckons to you to follow him. He calls to his wife that he'll be at work with the boy down below. You can't remember him ever addressing you as Charlie. To him you're "the boy," or "Karl" at best.

When an unskilled and uninterested person like you enters a hobbyist's workshop, he feels like he's visiting a leper colony. Everything's dirty, there are machines standing around everywhere, you bump into metal objects and bruise yourself. The place reeks of oil, it's drafty, and in the midst of this unpleasant clutter stands the squinting Bonesetter, his face aglow with pride.

As if you've never been here before, the Bonesetter takes you on a guided tour. He rests his hirsute hand on various contraptions and gives you an elaborate account of what they're used for. Every now and then he picks up a cup and takes a noisy slurp of coffee. You still haven't had any, but you refrain from mentioning the fact.

Having done due justice to his equipment, the Bonesetter is satisfied. His favorite folk ensemble is Die Fidelen Mölltaler. He turns them on full blast and proceeds to attack an old electric stove with a screwdriver.

You stroll around with one hand in your pants pocket, the other surreptitiously rubbing your eyes. There's nothing in sight that could genuinely interest you.

Now and then the Bonesetter bellows an order. You jump to it and hand him some tool or other. Before long there are oil stains on your pants and you're disgusted to find that your fingernails are in mourning.

In the intervals between folk songs, the Bonesetter asks why you're whimpering like that. Have you hurt yourself? You tell him you aren't whimpering at all.

PULL YOURSELF TOGETHER

All this takes a long time, and it isn't exactly fun. You're even glad when the Bonesetter's wife comes clattering down the stairs in her clogs to ask her husband if everything's all right. Seizing the opportunity, he sends you running around during the thirty seconds she spends in the cellar. It's like undergoing a speed drill. For all that, the presence of his wife, who looks as if she weighs a bit more than you do, makes a change from your stupefying incarceration with the Bonesetter.

To the tune of "America" from *West Side Story*, you sing:

> *I am the Bonesetter's prisoner,*
> *his most unfortunate prisoner,*
> *there's nothing I can do to get out*
> *of this detestable dungeeeon!*

Carried away by sheer exuberance, you give vent to more and more outrageous crescendi:

> *There's nothing I can do to get out*
> *of this detestable dungeeeooon!*

The Bonesetter turns the stereo system down, squints past you, and asks, "What's the matter with you?"

Hours go by. The Bonesetter is still tinkering with his stove and explaining things you've forgotten even before he's finished his sentence. You have to do this and that, hurry here and there, hand him this screwdriver or that pair of pliers, press this button or throw that switch.

Meantime, you think of all sorts of things. Whether to acquire a pet, for instance. On the plus side for a dog is its faithful nature. But do you really want to traipse to the nearest lamppost every morning, every night, and in every kind of weather? A cat would be better from that point of view, but cats are supposed to be contrary creatures. A hamster, maybe? Hamsters spend all night running inside their wheels and sleep by day. They smell, though. A lot of people keep rats too.

"Yes, that button there," the Bonesetter says ungraciously, pointing to a switch on the wall.

You shrug your shoulders. A switch is a switch, not a button, but who wants to debate linguistic niceties with an irascible Bonesetter? You flip the switch, there's a sizzling sound, and the Bonesetter breathes his last.

NOTE TO SELF: If you subject a man to a powerful electric current, he'll die. Even if he is a doctor of sorts.

A lthough you've already had experience of the law thanks to your mother's various escapades, this doesn't do you much good when you're the person who's being grilled by the hard-nosed guys in Homicide. It doesn't occur to you to invent things or lie in that sort of situation. Their faces register brutal resolve, and were it not for the presence of Inspector Trautmannsdorf, a gruff but kindly old cop, you'd be wetting yourself in front of everyone.

"He told you to press the button, but a switch isn't a button."

"That's what I said to myself: a switch is a switch, not a button."

"But you threw the switch. There's no button anywhere near that switch."

"I know. I wasn't thinking. My thoughts were elsewhere. I was wondering whether to buy a dog."

"You impudent brat," bellows one of the men with brutish features, driving his forefinger into your stomach. "Are you trying to give us the runaround, you tub of lard?"

"If I might be allowed to explain…"

"A switch is a switch," says another man in the background. "It isn't a button."

When you get into the newspapers because you've inadvertently barbecued a friend of the family, it isn't the pleasantest of publicity and certainly not the fame you've always dreamed of. Newshounds call and ask for details. You're scared of going to prison. The lawyer Aunt Kathi is paying for talks of homicide, manslaughter, negligence, and accidental death until your head throbs.

That you eventually get off without even a court appearance you owe to a conscientious pathologist who examines the Bonesetter's squinting eyes and arrives at an estimated optical discrepancy of five yards.

An on-the-spot examination of the workshop corroborates all the statements you've made. There's a button located five yards from the switch.

"You see, sergeant?" says Inspector Trautmannsdorf. "All's well that ends well."

"Is a switch a switch, or is it a button?"

"Come on now, anyone's thoughts can wander occasionally."

"But they don't always fry someone."

NOTE TO SELF: If you inadvertently kill someone without evil intent, those of your acquaintances who are devoted to cannabis consumption and Indian religions give you a wide berth because, in their eyes, you're a karmically compromised individual.

When a German talk show invites you to discuss the Bonesetter's accidental death, you take a long time making up your mind. You're as often on the point of refusing as you are of picking up the phone and accepting.

If you're listening to some good music with your head-phones on, you imagine how successful such a program could be. Everyone is sympathetic and finds you attractive and inter-esting, women gaze at you languishingly in the studio, newspa-pers print your picture and write about the fascinating young Austrian who has conquered Germany in double-quick time. At home you're recognized on the street and accosted by friendly strangers. In restaurants you always get a table and free beer, the proprietors being proud of your patronage. You're pestered for autographs. Film and television jobs beckon. You appear at Rock at the Ring with Phillip Boa and sing duets with other celebs. You're universally popular and become a superstar. You fly Mom in for a concert and meet her in the penthouse suite of the five-star hotel you're treating her to. She stands there open-mouthed.

Soon after you remove the headphones, your euphoria starts to subside. Doubt gnaws you. In such cases it's wise to steer clear of the phone for a while and thereby avoid refusing.

After you've sent the Bonesetter to the happy hunting grounds, Aunt Kathi refrains from recommending her great-nephew to any more influential people. She posthumously berates the Bonesetter for leaving you only eighty thousand schillings in his will.

"But Aunt," Mom objects, "Charlie killed him."

"He couldn't have known that in advance! He was still alive when he made his will!"

She remains impervious to all arguments. So embittered is she by the Bonesetter's gross undervaluation of her great-nephew that she no longer invites his widow to her home—indeed, she declines even to acknowledge her when they meet on the street.

Aunt Kathi absolves you from attending the funeral. You beat your brains about the legacy. It's dirty money, as they say in heist movies; then again, it would come in handy.

You go to the lawyer's office and sign a receipt for it. For a while, though, you sleep with the light on because you're scared the Bonesetters's ghost may come and avenge him. Your bad conscience about the dumb switch that was a button makes it hard for you to go to sleep. At night you sit up with a start and peer around the room for fear the Bonesetter is standing there, squinting malignly at you.

You're surprised to receive a letter whose neutral-looking envelope suggests that it isn't a bill.

You're even more surprised when you open it. It's from the married couple whose ad in the porn magazine you replied to, in an alarming state of horniness, a considerable time ago. You occasionally hoped rather than thought that you'd never hear from them, and now they've replied after all.

You're informed that you're cordially invited by the "red-hot married slut plus husband" to spend an "informal evening" at their home for the purpose of "getting to know each other." Should "mutual attraction" result, "no holds" would be barred. The husband would "merely watch."

Wow, you think.

While you're wondering what to do, the phone rings. In an absurd fit of paranoia you're afraid it may be your new pen pals. It isn't the married slut, however, but Aunt Kathi, who showers you with reproaches. Not content with your obvious lack of achievement at the university, you neglect your darling mother and the Aunticles and never bring them flowers.

NOTE TO SELF: If you're being subjected to increasing pressure from all quarters, it's best to go to a pet store and acquire a three-month-old black cat.

The animal is a lady cat. You christen her Mimi on the spot. You also buy her a litter tray, several cans of feline baby food, and some toys and crockery. Then you bring her home in the basket you've also acquired.

Since Mimi seems rather bewildered by her change of location, you leave her in peace after preparing her a comfortable nest and serving her a meal. You turn the television on low. Unable to restrain yourself from time to time, you crawl over to the kitten and stroke her, entranced by the cute way in which she washes herself, sniffs your outstretched hand, plays with her own tail, and skitters after a piece of string. She turns somersaults, knocks over some glasses lying on the floor, meow, purrs, and cavorts around. A good thing Nero isn't there. You can just imagine how the lecherous little brute would have pounced on her.

You're so carried away by the kitten's appearance on the scene, you skip a planned visit to the Jack Point. Instead, you ask Mirko to drop in. When he hears about Mimi, he agrees. He's a cat lover too.

NOTE TO SELF: Being somewhat distracted after acquiring a cat, you may leave things lying around that ought to be concealed from the eyes of others.

"Hey, don't tell me you replied to an ad like this!" cries Mirko, brandishing the letter.

He gives you no peace until you've come clean.

"Well, what do you propose to do?"

"Nothing. Throw the letter away—burn the thing, preferably, and forget I ever received it."

"The hell you will!" Mirko exclaims. "Here, look"—he takes a sheet of paper and starts writing—"Dear married slut, I'd be delighted to 'come'…"

He smirks to himself, and his agility and physical superiority make it impossible for you to snatch the paper away. Undeterred, he forges your handwriting and signature. Having written the married slut's address on an envelope and stamped it, he inserts the letter and dashes out the apartment. You set off in hot pursuit, but there's no stopping him, either by tugging at his jacket or by yelling threats. He shoves the envelope into the mailbox, then hugs you and laughs.

Back in the apartment, you flop down on the bed in a state of resignation and apathetically watch Mirko's hands becoming acquainted with the kitten's claws.

When you pay Aunt Ernestine a visit at midday on December 24 and present her with a shoebox-size model of a Mercedes 600, she's as touched as if you'd gone to the infinite trouble of knitting her a sweater. The Mercedes 600 is her favorite automobile.

Her gift to you is an envelope. The nature of its contents isn't in doubt. The only question is, how many thousand-schilling bills will it be this time?

She proposes to make some coffee. You take over the job yourself and wash up the cups afterward. She's been a bit unsteady on her legs for several weeks now. This makes you nervous. You can imagine what it may mean but you're reluctant to accept the possibility. Losing Aunt Ernestine would be the greatest misfortune you can conceive of.

When an elderly member of the family is on her way out, you notice it in her demeanor. Aunt Ernestine has quieted down. You often sense her watching you. She sits there gazing at you intently. It seems she's pondering what will become of you when she isn't there anymore. She's getting ready.

Early that evening, when you get to the Auncticles' house for the Christmas Eve festivities, one glance at the assembled guests tells you that disaster is inevitable. Everyone is there. Mom, the Auncticles, Uncle Hans, and Aunt Wilma. Also invited are the family's new best friends, because that, in Aunt Kathi's opinion, is only fitting: a respectable family invites good friends of the family to Christmas present giving. This applies to the Sedlaks, who greet you politely but with a certain reserve. You don't know much about the couple. She carries a rosary wherever she goes, he's an insurance salesman.

At one unobserved moment, you loosen your tie. You look around. Everyone is wearing suits and the mandatory carpet slippers.

At eight p.m. precisely, a bell rings. Sentimental Aunt Wilma puts the "Silent Night" record on and everyone breaks into song. Since no one in the room possesses a voice or an ear for music, a medley of squawks and whimpers rings out in front of the Christmas tree. Tears of emotion are visible nonetheless. You can't help reflecting that this is the first Christmas Eve for years on which no girl will be expecting you later. The lump in your throat you've been feeling all day grows thicker.

Uncle Hans, the only person in the gathering who seems to understand you, gives you a surreptitious pat on the back.

Once the singing has died away, everyone kisses and wishes each other a happy Christmas. Gifts are exchanged.

It's been agreed for years that the family won't give presents, and for years they've all turned up with them. It's only a little thing, they say. If you've kept to the agreement you stand there looking stupid, so Christmas presents have to be obtained.

It's an immutable rule that the approach of Christmas makes you more and more nervous every day. This is because you've no idea what to give to whom. It's clear that nobody ever likes what they're given, just as you yourself don't delight in T-shirts with Bambi motifs or checked briefcases, so Uncle Johann gets the same wine as the year before, Aunt Kathi the same perfume, Mom another china ornament for her display cabinet, Aunt Wilma another pantyhose, and Uncle Hans an autographed photo of Heinz Kinigartner, the motocross star. He's the only one whose gratitude is unfeigned. The Sedlaks get a handshake.

Everyone gives you money envelopes, as they do every year, the sole exception being Mom. She has gotten you some face cream from Holland because your complexion certainly won't improve without it, she says, and you look like a sow after a hormone cure. You thank her unenthusiastically. Aunt Kathi scolds you over your shoulder. You're an ungrateful boy, she hisses, and should be glad of such expensive face cream.

For those sitting down at the table on December 24, Christmas dinner has always, from time immemorial, consisted of spaghetti Bolognese and potato salad. Since Aunt Kathi's culinary skills have undergone absolutely no change since the straitened days of World War Two, the pasta is a mass of mush with a blancmange-like substance quivering on top of it. As for the potato salad, it bears only a distant qualitative resemblance to the stuff at the Jack Point.

Family matters are discussed over this infernal repast.

When Uncle Johann wipes his lips on his napkin, it signals that everyone is at liberty to behave more informally.

You go and sit on the toilet, tear a couple of strips off the roll, and stuff them in your ears to muffle the voices from the living room. You sing "The End" to yourself and lapse into a daydream.

You've accepted the talk show invitation after all and are now a celeb. Paoletta ditches her actor and quits her archaeology course because she insists on attending every concert you give and follows you halfway across Germany. You confront her in a hotel lobby. She mustn't throw her life away for an obsession, you tell her; her feelings for you may be strong, but she mustn't give up on herself. She should resume her studies and you'll come and see her when you're back in town. Bursting into sobs, she says she can't bear to wait that long. She wants to stay—she can't imagine life without you. Why can't you sleep with her, at least? With a smile, you tell her it's not possible. You dab the tears from her cheeks…

The hammering on the bathroom door is audible even through your toilet paper earplugs. It's so vigorous, you jump up and pluck them out of your ears.

"What's all that wailing?" Mom yells. "Did you fall asleep in there? D'you think you're the only one who needs a—"

"Don't say it!" says Aunt Kathi's voice. "Don't you dare! Not in this house!"

With your Christmas loot in your pocket, you can afford a cab. You take one to the Café Schiller. It's shut. The cabby informs you that bars are forbidden to open on Christmas Eve; the government wants men to spend the holiday with their families instead of getting drunk. He does, however, know of two establishments that disobey this regulation.

The guy might have told me that before, you think.

"Okay, let's go."

If you're a wimp, you say nothing when you're short-changed in a store. Every week.

If you're a wimp, you say nothing when you're cheated in the vegetable market. Seldom.

If you're a wimp, you say nothing when the butcher sells you rancid salami. Often.

If you're a wimp, you say nothing when a cabby takes you for a ride. Every week.

If you're a wimp, restaurants fob you off with tough meat and stale rolls. And you say nothing. Every day.

Contrary to a view widespread among older people, disreputable establishments like the Priamus are extremely beneficial to a young man's development. The Priamus is a place where pimps, whores, artists, and students mingle and all kinds of splendid things happen. People are occasionally threatened with guns, brawls can break out, and the police show up there every other day. A young man with no intention of becoming a lawyer or an accountant should patronize such premises at least three times a week.

If you witness an incident like one of these, you sit quaking in a corner, mortally afraid of getting mixed up in anything. When it's all over, you casually ask around to find out what it was about. The next day, you can boast of your adventure to friends who never venture into such dangerous drinking dens.

The Priamus is almost deserted this Christmas Eve. Fritz, the owner, says this is normal but he keeps the place open anyway.

Undeterred by the threat of a fine, he's proud of never having closed for a single day in seven years.

When you spot a whore you once accosted on the opposite side of the bar, you act like you don't know her. Although you're still proud of that conversation—how many people can boast of being on nodding terms with a member of the so-called underworld?—you don't feel like talking to her now. It was fun to brush up against the so-called demimonde when you were above it all, but tonight, when you're feeling not only agonizingly lonely but closer to these people than your relations and former friends, you want nothing to do with the solitary whore.

In such a situation, it's best to order yourself a hot chocolate and read the sports pages.

NOTE TO SELF: When you feel you're going downhill fast, it's nice to have a cat waiting for you back home.

B ecause your experiences of the last few days have made an impression on you, you pull yourself together and devote the week before New Year's to your books. You resolve to enter for the next round of examinations. You feel you're stuck in a morass and sinking steadily deeper. That's not what you want. You want to belong to the good guys and live in the light of day. You don't want to belong in the Priamus. If you go there at all, you want to do so like a rubbernecking tourist, then go home and rejoice in your different perspectives.

Two days before New Year's your enthusiasm wanes. More and more often, you lay aside the massive tome you're working your way through, pick up *Old Surehand I*, and gorge yourself on burgers, French fries, peanut-butter sandwiches, candies, waffles, sausage, chips, and chocolate. Art history bores you. What's more, you've now grasped that not every art history graduate becomes a professor or a museum director. So you wonder if it isn't time to apply the emergency brake.

Many emergency brakes are well concealed.

If you wake up on New Year's Eve feeling rather apprehensive, it's because the married slut and her husband are expecting you this evening. Mirko, the scheming bastard, has fixed this date and insists you keep it. You'd far rather celebrate New Year's with him at the Socialist Students' club.

In such a situation, you're well advised to lie on your bed and masturbate. This relieves you of a certain tension and will disappoint the married slut. You call Mirko and tell him, very firmly, that you won't meet with that couple under any circumstances; you'll accompany him to the club instead.

"Okay," says Mirko. "I'll pick you up just before eight."

NOTE TO SELF: Asserting yourself generates a feeling of satisfaction and inner serenity.

Having drunk a glass of wine at home at five p.m., you feed Mimi at five thirty and drink another glass. Because you pour yourself another glass at six and the next one follows it ten minutes later, you greet Mirko, who's waiting in the taxi, in an unusually relaxed frame of mind.

He smiles at you, and before you know it you're in a headlock.

"Now take us to the address I gave you!" Mirko calls to the cabby.

You think he's joking. For a while you simultaneously laugh and threaten him, but the longer the trip lasts the more you realize he's in earnest and there's no escaping his viselike grip. You resort to entreaties. You hear the cabby laughing. It won't hurt just to look in on those people, Mirko retorts.

NOTE TO SELF: When you're hauled out of a cab by an unpredictable and physically superior friend, you limit your resistance to rhetoric.

Mirko drags you up the steps by the scruff of your neck and runs his finger down the nameplates. He takes you up to the third floor and rings the bell. Not until footsteps are heard does he let you go and vault over the banisters onto the landing below.

You're envious when you see how agile a slim person can be.

"You must be Rubens," says the married slut, extending her hand.

The first time you meet a married couple who place ads in pornographic magazines, you're surprised to find that they're neither overweight nor averse to personal hygiene. Not that they're beauties. The husband's neck and forearms are sprinkled with dark birthmarks, but he could look worse. They're normal-looking individuals. You couldn't describe them as repulsive. You'd been prepared for anything, but not this.

The husband, who introduces himself as Leo, shakes your hand. He looks you in the eye as he does so, then indicates a bottle of prosecco. You nod.

The married slut's name is Hilde. She has a big pigmentation mark on her forehead just above the right eye. Hilde is around the same age as her husband. Early forties. She smells of perfume. She's neither provocatively dressed nor overly made up. You're thankful for that.

The moment before the door opened, you'd meant to take a look at the couple and then split, but Mirko was probably waiting downstairs and would stop you making a getaway. On top of that, you find you really wouldn't mind going to bed with Hilde after all.

Leo asks what you do for a living. Aha, he says, a student; Hilde likes students. He glances at his wife and smiles.

Not knowing how to respond to this promising intro, which makes your heart pound, you ask the same question of your hosts. Leo says he owns a leather business and his wife keeps the books.

"Aha," you say.

Leo seems to be a nervous type. He keeps twisting something in his hands and never stays still for a moment.

"Mind if I slip into something more comfortable," he asks, "and then put some music on?"

"Not at all."

He gets up and goes next door. Hilde comes closer. She pours you a glass of prosecco.

"Ever answered an ad before?"

You say no. She nods as if she'd expected that. You register you're being inspected from head to toe. She looks friendly. Not like a married slut at all.

Leo returns wearing a kimono. His legs and chest are also sprinkled with birthmarks. He and his wife exchange glances. He clears his throat.

"Oh, let's forget about the music."

He goes into another adjacent room and reappears with four videocassettes in his hand.

"Do you have any special tastes?" he inquires.

——— - ———

Because general uncertainty leads to nightmares, you obtain a spare key to Aunt Ernestine's house on some pretext. You often dream of her and are scared she may be telepathically summoning help. In the middle of the night you take a cab to the outskirts of town and check to see if she's still breathing. The very thought that she may be dying makes you feel physically sick.

With rising panic, you scan the job offers. You fondle Mimi and despair of ever finding a job. You don't want to go into insurance, nor would you ever consider working as a gas station attendant. Offers such as 100% HOME-BASED SIDELINE! sound interesting. When you call, you discover that they involve sealing envelopes or pyramid schemes.

One particular ad catches your eye: SECURITY GUARDS FOR CONCERTS WANTED. At length, after ruminatively pacing up and down for an entire day, you chuck the newspaper away. Nothing would come of it. If you can't handle Mirko, how could you expect to see off a bunch of freaked-out rock fans?

While stroking Mimi's purring form and consuming a gas station tiramisu, you wonder what talents you possess. You get out a sheet of paper and a pencil.

I can drive a car.

After three hours, that's still the extent of the list.

The thought of employment by Meals on Wheels or a cab company makes your toes curl. You had other ambitions. They're incompatible with being a gofer and fighting for financial survival.

So what?

Drive a cab. Deliver meals to senior citizens. Donate blood. Go from door to door. Become a hotel porter, a warehouseman, a waiter. Sell insurance.

NOTE TO SELF: The decision to make a serious attempt at self-knowledge always coincides with spells of low morale and profound intellectual depression.

You resolve to study hard. You'll discover who you are, what you can do, and what you want. You still have time, even one of the superannuated artists at the Priamus assured you of that. You have time till you're twenty-five, but after that you have to put on speed; there are too many failures and windbags and drink-sodden idlers around. You're still a long way short of twenty-five. You don't have to earn money yet, you get it given you. Blessed be the givers. There's no need to be anxious, but you've got to get a grip on yourself.

The euphoria engendered by your decision to make a fresh start brings tears to your eyes. Feeling relieved and happy, you go to the bookstore to acquire some background reading. For the first time in ages, you walk past the lifestyle guides and home in on the philosophy section. You take some Kant, Fromm, and Nietzsche from the shelf.

On the way to the cash desk, you can't resist inspecting the new additions to the lifestyle guides. *The Path to Self-Awareness*? You've never seen that one before. You take it with you.

Having paid, you feel better. You've made a start. You won't screw it up or become a failure and windbag.

When you're standing on the street with some books by Kant and Fromm under your arm and freezing your toes off in your cool new boots, you're convinced you've earned a visit to the Jack Point. Although a bus is going that way, you hail a cab. You still have enough Christmas money left.

After eating four portions of potato salad, you fall on the slot machines like a maniac. You play pinball. You play table football with a taciturn Serb. You reach the final of the world basketball championship. You sit in the flight simulator until you're giddy. The jinxed fiver machine swallows seventy fivers.

You finally feel that's enough. You take a cab to the Café Schiller to read some Kant.

Among the cultural achievements of the nineties is a man's right to wear pantyhose. After spending several hours in an ill-heated amusement arcade, you're annoyed with yourself for having renounced that right today. Your feet are like ice, and it doesn't help being fat. If you're already in the process of reshaping your life, maybe you should take up a sport.

Even before ordering a coffee in the Café Schiller, you remove one of the books from the bag.

NOTE TO SELF: The first time you embark on a book by Kant, you don't know what's hit you.

Having discovered that Kant is too tough to cut your teeth on, you experience an instant desire for a slice of Black Forest gâteau and feel annoyed you don't have a Karl May with you. You go over to the newspaper rack and get yourself a *Kronen Zeitung.* Delighted to have spotted the five mistakes in the picture puzzle right away, you immerse yourself in the sports section.

The waitress appears. And then something wonderful happens.

You've often tried to imagine what your next girlfriend will look like. There are times when you stand in a men's room, drunkenly wondering what the girl in question, who's still a total stranger to you, is doing at that moment. She may be peeling potatoes or sashaying across a disco dance floor, or she may just have had some disappointing sex with her future ex-boyfriend.

Considerations of this kind can even sneak up on you while you yourself are still in a relationship. On the principle of here today, gone tomorrow, you speculate about the girl-friend in store for you. And when you're sitting half-frozen in the Café Schiller, reading the *Kronen Zeitung,* you've sus-pected for quite a while that the next woman you fall in love with will be a waitress. Especially since you never get to know any other girls. When you do meet her, though, you're speech-less. Your heart races. You gaze at her with your mouth open.

"Are you in pain?" she asks. "Or wasn't it you that made that whimpering noise?"

You're receptive when you're in love.

You hate it as a rule when Mom smuggles diet pills and ointments into your laundry bag, but you have to look acceptable when trying to make a conquest. If you had the money, you'd even have some cosmetic surgery done to your face.

Because Laura keeps you dangling and you don't want to make a fool of yourself by sitting at the counter of the Café Schiller from morning to night, you devote yourself to the intensive enhancement of your mind, body, and character. In the mornings you do three push-ups. Whenever you remember, at least. You feed and stroke Mimi, then walk to the nearest café for breakfast. Eggs, toast, ham, rolls, butter, marmalade. You overtip the waiter because you're afraid he may take a disliking to you.

On the way home you buy yourself a *Kronen Zeitung*. Although you wouldn't read such a rag in public, it's an indispensable aid to keeping up with developments in the worlds of politics and sports.

That job done, you watch television. Later, you open a couple of cans, although you've already had your fill of Inzersdorfer's frankfurters in goulash sauce.

Early in the afternoon you take a shower. Groomed and fortified in this manner, you open the Fromm and further your education.

You're firmly convinced that some book in this world can tell you who you are, what you want to be, and what you should do.

You still don't realize, alas, that this will entail reading a host of books, none of which will bring you any nearer your objective.

When you go to the Schiller early that evening and Laura isn't there as you'd expected, you're dumbfounded. You've looked forward to seeing her all day long. Counted the hours. Rehearsed turns of phrase. Imagined yourself kissing her.

You sit down, order a coffee from an unknown waiter, and try to picture Laura. Unsuccessfully.

NOTE TO SELF: When you're in love, you can't recall your beloved's face.

You know Laura is dark-haired and dark-eyed. She's petite. She wears stainless-steel rings and a thin leather necklace. She always wears jeans. The swell of her breasts can be glimpsed beneath her blouse. She sometimes smells musty, like she lives in a basement apartment. You know all the details, but you still can't picture her features.

If, contrary to what you expect, you fail to see your beloved, it's advisable to call Mirko and ask him to join you.

You have a glass of wine while waiting. You have several more glasses. You become euphoric. Someone turns the music up. You click your fingers, hum along, shut your eyes, and picture yourself and Laura in a dangerous situation.

An armed man has raided the café. A maniac, he takes Laura and all of the customers hostage. He negotiates with the police by phone. To underline his threats he shoots a woman and an elderly man. Everyone is panic-stricken and horrified. You alone remain completely unruffled. You've acted from the first as if you're mentally retarded. You sit there waggling your head, drooling, uttering guttural sounds, and waiting for an opportune moment. Laura's eyes beseech you not to try anything that could endanger you.

When the hostage-taker walks past you, you spring to your feet and karate-chop the nape of his neck so hard, he falls dead.

The police arrive. People hug one another and express their thanks. You wave them away. It was nothing special, you say. Laura gazes at you admiringly. You go over to the people who were shot. Kneeling down beside them, you close their eyes and say, "Sorry I couldn't do more for you."

You're jolted out of this daydream by Mirko, who thumps you on the back and asks why you're twitching that way.

You have to tell him about Laura even before he gets his first glass of wine. Then you enlighten him about the new life you're utterly determined to lead. Idleness and amusement arcades are the devil's work. One has to confront life with vigor and intelligence, you say. Life is a challenge.

"And you're a moron," says Mirko. "Let's go to the Jack Point."

"Only if we take a cab," you reply.

NOTE TO SELF: Pursuing an objective is hard if you don't know what it is.

Because Mimi, the Jack Point, the *Kronen Zeitung*, the Priamus, and Laura are more congenial to you than Kant, Fromm, Sartre, art history, cooking lessons, and push-ups, certain of your lofty objectives lapse into oblivion.

You sometimes look in on your old friends in the students' association and more than once let yourself be talked into smoking a joint with them. When a new machine is installed at the Jack Point, you allow yourself the luxury of playing on it until you've mastered the highest level. In your capacity as a mute but tolerated customer of the Priamus, you listen for nights on end to toothless artists expatiating on their blueprints for society and theories of art. No one can claim you aren't furthering your education by doing this. Consorting with artists is a worthy and revitalizing occupation. Who cares if they're over fifty, pour beer and schnapps down their throats by the quart, and are total unknowns?

From time to time, however, you notice certain ominous signs.

The FIST chairman has nicotine stains on his ring finger and little finger.

At the Jack Point you overhear a conversation between two regulars in which you're referred to as "The Reverend."

You only wear moccasins these days because your gut gets in the way and it hurts when you bend over, so tying shoelaces is beyond you.

Because you sit stewing in the Priamus too often and for too long, Mimi protestingly craps in the bathtub.

You've taken out a subscription to the *Kronen Zeitung*.

You know whole scenes from Part One of *The Godfather* by heart and recite them under the shower to the tune of "Knowing Me, Knowing You" as you wash your genitals without looking.

When one continually reaches a dead end, one longs for new options. Since Laura is one such option, her reluctance to embark on an affair with you is doubly painful. You seek refuge in poetry. You go around with a long face until you learn from a lifestyle guide that men with a feeble aura are unattractive to women. And so, dumping your volumes of poetry in the leather briefcase you're never without, you read *What the Eyes Reveal* instead.

"You need money as much as I do. Come with me. But none of the others must know."

The FIST chairman mashes out his cigarette against the wall and looks around like he's scared of secret agents. You're standing with him outside the door of the Socialist Students' bar. He has just suggested you accompany him to Germany for a few weeks to drum up donations for the Red Cross. He did this during the last summer vacation and earned a mint of money, but his comrades mustn't find out. He prefers that they go on believing that he worked his ass off as a volunteer on a kibbutz.

"I couldn't possibly do that," you tell him.

"Yes, even you could. You go from door to door, look friendly, and persuade people to transfer a certain monthly sum from their bank account to the Red Cross. It's dead easy. They're Germans! They've got a bad conscience! They're generous!"

"Oh, I don't know…"

He lights his next cigarette, a Cuban weed brought back from the last solidarity trip to Havana, and peers over his shoulder again. He confides how much he earned in six weeks last summer. You open your eyes.

"Yessir," he laughs. "And there'll be two of us, don't forget. It'll be a gas."

You promise to think it over. You know you'll turn him down, of course. Leave home? For several weeks? Take off into the blue? Brrr! And leave Laura behind? For a while now, she's been brushing up against you as if by accident and taking you by the arm. She seems to like you letting her order you around, carry heavy crates of beer for her, and not minding when she calls you a dumbbell and puts you down in front of other people. Do without her for the sake of money? You'd sooner live on bread and water. Besides, your eighty-thousand-schilling legacy will come through soon.

When you're in dire financial straits and expecting a remittance, you swallow your pangs of conscience and pay a daily visit to the bank to inquire if the money has finally come through. You don't want it because you sent its former owner to kingdom come, but you need it. You have to deal with the situation. You're in debt. Debt! All that cash you've been withdrawing from the ATM—the bank wants it back!

Besides, you've seen some cool boots in a store window. You'd like to invite Laura to dine at a ritzy restaurant. As for the Afghan black the FIST people keep raving about, you'd like to try some at your leisure. At least once. And for that you'll need some suitable music. You'll thank providence for these gifts by means of scholarly endeavor.

When you're out of the red at last, you call Mirko and ask him to keep you company on a shopping trip.

You see the boots you think are really smart, so you buy two pairs at once. It so happens that a bomber jacket catches your eye in the next store along. Some new pants are essential, so you don't economize in the jeans boutique either.

From there you go to a record store. You simply must have the latest Blumfeld album. And a few other things. You've made out a list. You buy, buy, buy. Mirko picks out some CDs he thinks are good. You buy them just to please him. If they're no good, you'll make him a present of them.

NOTE TO SELF: There are few more restorative things in the world than a shopping trip with plenty of cash to throw around.

Walking down the street laden with shopping bags, you bump into the scar-faced girl you met at Edith's election party. Since the test in *Personality* categorizes you as an 87 percent wimp, an 82 percent conformist, and a 56 percent trickster, but only a 10 percent shoulder-shrugger and a 3 percent adventurer, you don't say what you'd like to say, which is: Would you care to join us for a coffee?

"Would you care to join us for a coffee?"

Says Mirko.

"Why not?"

Says the scar-faced girl.

Her name is Conny. She doesn't have much to do with the FIST people anymore, preferring to concentrate on her pharmacy course. She earns money by writing instruction leaflets. Fiddling with her silver necklace, she asks what you yourself have been up to. Mirko, whom you told about the girl and who enjoys playing the matchmaker, uncharacteristically takes a back seat and gives you an encouraging kick under the table.

When a passionate do-nothing is asked, straight out, how he earns his living, he ought to save face by denying the questioner an answer of any kind.

Luckily, you're able to impress the slender-fingered girl by disclosing that you divide your time between studying, stroking your cat, and reading Erich Fromm. Conny laughs. This enables you to convey the cup of coffee to your lips on the third attempt without spilling any.

For a while you try flirting, a form of social intercourse in which you're less than adequately able to engage with a maliciously smirking friend seated beside you. You frown at him to get lost but the bastard doesn't take the hint. In the end, Conny has to go. You manage to exchange phone numbers and give her a farewell wave.

"There," says Mirko, "you see?"

You don't ask what he means by that. You sit down again. Mirko signals to the waitress to bring you two beers.

You subside into a daydream in which two unknown men drag Conny toward a car on the street. She struggles and cries for help. You stroll casually up, say, "Permit me!" and fell the first man with a hard right hook to the temple. The second man lets go of Conny and draws a switchblade. Chuckling evilly, he flourishes it around in front of you. You stick your hands in your pants pockets and grin at him. Conny looks on in dread. The man goes for you. You skillfully evade him and dance around, still with your hands in your pockets. A ring of spectators has formed. There!—the knife man lunges, presenting you with an opening. One kick, and the switchblade goes whirling through the air. He comes for you with his fists raised. You evade him with ease, laughing as you do so. Your kicks land again and again. He's bleeding and limping now. The spectators cheer. Little boys jeer at him.

NOTE TO SELF: When you're immersed in a daydream in a sidewalk café, you may quite inadvertently give the table you happen to be sitting at an elegant karate kick and send it flying in front of a passing car, thereby incurring universal indignation and displeasure.

H ilde isn't a slut, so she must have read too many porn mag-azines or it wouldn't have occurred to her to devise such a dumb description for herself. Hilde and Leo are an engaging couple and you like them. When you sit on their elephant-hide sofa, glass in hand, you ask yourself if what you do to and with them hurts anyone. But Leo made it clear from the outset that he never allowed himself to be dominated by physical jealousy. This, he said, is an almost indispensable strategy for life. In any event, it is if you want to lead a happy existence in which you deny yourself nothing.

"If you met Hilde on the side," he told me, "I'd give you a thrashing. If you do it here in front of me, I'm happy."

And he didn't mean even that the way he said it. Leo could never use violence on anyone. He's the gentlest person you've ever met.

NOTE TO SELF: When you get to know a couple of swingers well, you should make it a habit to temporarily postpone the real rea-son for your get-togethers and titillate one another by engaging in superficial, suggestive conversation.

Leo is a sexual theorist. He has a theory about everything. He says one must expand one's horizons, especially today, in an age devoid of ideology and meaning. And to that end, one shouldn't abstain from free-and-easy conversations about sex. Too many people in the world are too cowardly to obtain the gratification they secretly desire, and this unnecessary and dishonest form of self-castigation sooner or later turns such people into perverted brutes. Leo asserts that educators neglect two essential aspects of life: food and sex. If society isn't one day to consist of starving sadists, parents should be obliged to send their children out into the world with an in-depth knowledge of cooking and sexual behavior.

During the hour you spend in the apartment before Hilde asks you to oil her or go and get the video camera, you're continually amazed by your hosts' candor, but also by their imaginative turn of mind. That people should talk about their desires so uninhibitedly is something new in your experience. What you find particularly remarkable is that Hilde and Leo are normal individuals who tell you about the daily routine in their business. They know something of the world and are always ready with sound advice if you have problems.

When you mention your eighty-thousand-schilling legacy, Leo and Hilde sit up with a jerk. "You must invest it," Leo exclaims. "Buy some shares."

They both become insistent and persuasive. They name some financial institutions. Leo fetches a fountain pen and paper and writes down a bank expert's phone number. He's wearing nothing but a silk thong. Hilde is almost naked too.

Her breasts repose in a kind of transparent harness, and all she has on down below is a garter belt. Lecturing someone on financial transactions in such a getup is not only courageous but a source of secret amusement to you.

The discussion of your legacy doesn't end until Hilde suddenly announces that she's feeling like a sandwich. Her tone is so innocuous, there's a moment when you're genuinely tempted to go to the kitchen.

Humans being inquisitive by nature, you're always reaching stages in your life when you feel dissatisfied with your circle of friends and yearn for new faces and perspectives.

To get to know people, it's advisable to take Laura to an art-house movie theater and lean against the bar in the cafeteria. This kills two birds with one stone. For one thing, you prove to Laura that you're an intellectual with taste; for another, you're standing beside a bunch of movie freaks, who are the kind of people worth getting to know—even though a film buff is someone who's either too lazy or too stupid to read books (*A Psychological Study of the History of Rock Music*).

Intellectuals interested in the art of film are dressed either very smartly or very slovenly. Many of them manage to be both at once. They drink beer from the bottle. They discuss art without a regional accent. They like Jim Jarmusch, Amos Poe, Johanna Heer, and a host of other people you've never heard of. Butting in on such people's conversations brings you new friends and perspectives.

NOTE TO SELF: When you're accepted by people you feel inferior to, you're happy and you want to emulate them in every way. Until, sooner or later, you outgrow them too.

Because one of the movie intellectuals is incredibly handsome, you decide while still at the bar to let your hair grow. An intellectual who takes pride in himself is a free spirit and can wear his hair any way he likes.

You talk with the group after the screening as well. You discuss the movie with the good-looking guy. You listen to his opinion and then endorse his verdict, which was that the film was fantastic. The truth is, it bored you stiff. Since Laura was averse to necking, you had to watch it all the way through. You rave about the acting for a while.

"Charlie, would you kindly stop talking such bull? You'd do better to say nothing at all. And you, you with the long hair, you're ridiculous!"

You dry up like you've been bludgeoned on the head. You've known for some time that Laura has a sharp tongue. Now the movie intellectuals discover that too. She calls the men at the bar a bunch of dummies who don't have a clue about life; the movie, she declares, was about love. Blushing furiously with your hands in your pockets, you wait till she's through.

Being a 3 percent adventurer means there are situations in which you discover that's precisely what you are.

Hands buried in the pockets of your jacket, you silently set off to find a restaurant with Laura. It's misty. Cars are driving along the rain-swept street with a monotonous hiss. You've no idea where to go, so you leave the choice to Laura.

When idiots own dogs, their dogs often look equally moronic. Small, degenerate animals as a rule, they're employed by their owners as mobile houseplants. You encounter an extreme variant of this type of pet some two hundred yards from the movie theater.

A man is walking his dog, an Airedale terrier, on a leash. Although the dog itself doesn't look moronic, it's wearing clothes. Its body is swathed in some red checked material resembling a Scottish kilt. Its paws, too, are encased in cloth—white cloth this time, which makes it look like it's wearing gloves. It also sports a denim jacket of more modern cut than anything hanging in your own closet at home. On its head is a tam-o'-shanter with a flower stuck in it.

When you encounter a dog that's being abused by its owner, you feel so sorry for the creature, the 3 percent adventurer in you momentarily overpowers the 87 percent wimp.

You go up to the dog owner and slap his face twice, once with each hand.

"You ought to be ashamed of yourself," you say, "treating a dog like this."

The man looks flabbergasted for a moment. Then he slaps you back—so hard that your glasses fly off and you sit down abruptly. Your two rather halfhearted slaps were intended more as a gesture, whereas his response could not be construed as such.

"This isn't my fucking dog!" he snarls, glaring down at you. "I'm being paid to walk the brute. You think this getup is *my* idea?"

"Nutcase," he adds. And he walks on, dragging the dog behind him.

You rub your smarting cheek. Laura picks up your glasses. She puts out her hand to help you up, but you're too heavy for her and have to struggle to your feet unaided.

"Maybe that wasn't altogether…"

She grins. "No, maybe it wasn't."

NOTE TO SELF: One shouldn't believe all one thinks.

When Laura kisses you on the way from the movie theater to a restaurant, it takes your breath away.

Interestingly enough, you don't think of going to bed with her right away. You're quite simply overjoyed by what she's allowing you to do. It really is exciting enough to fondle the new breasts and buttocks, stroke the new head. With your cheek still smarting, you stand at an intersection and smooch. Right now, you can't imagine doing anything beyond that. It's the ne plus ultra of happiness.

At last.

When you're smooching with your beloved for the first time and, just at that moment, Aunt Kathi walks past on the way home from her weekly game of cards, you're rather caught off balance.

"*So* in love? Who is the young lady?"

It's hard to find an appropriate answer in such circumstances. You look at the astonished old lady. You look at astonished Laura. Before you can collect your thoughts, Aunt Kathi laughs, pats you on the head, and says she's glad her great-nephew is doing well. You smell the wine on her breath when she kisses you.

Then and there she reaches in her purse, fishes out a hundred-schilling bill, and stuffs it in your pocket. You'd better get into the warm, she says. Some nice hot tea, perhaps. It's chilly, and one can so easily catch cold.

"Au revoir, Fräulein, nice to have met you."

And she waddles off. Laura stares at you.

You can't think what the consequences of this encounter may be. Laura asks who the old lady was.

"Can we talk about something else?" you reply.

You stroll on with her for a minute or two.

"What do you live on, actually?" asks Laura.

Thanks a bunch, dear Aunt, you think, but aloud you say:

"Investments."

Mom, brightly, when you bring her your dirty laundry: "What's this I hear? You've a new girlfriend?"

No decent person would dream of discussing love and sex with a parent. Quite apart from the embarrassment of it, you might run the risk of learning details of your parent's own love life, and that, by God, is the very last thing on earth you want to hear. So you try with the aid of gestures, grimaces, and sighs to impress on Mom that you're loath to talk about your private life.

"You can tell me. She isn't all that pretty, Aunt Kathi says, but she seemed nice. Go on, do tell…"

You make a dismissive gesture and reject all further inquiries with a shake of the head. You take an unobtrusive look around. Mom seems to be doing better lately. The apartment is tidier. There aren't as many empty bottles lying around. You hear and see no sign of any undesirable male acquaintances.

You dump your clean laundry in a sports bag. There's a fresh packet of diet pills on top of the pile. You draw Mom's attention to the fact that you won't swallow the unhealthy stuff. It wouldn't hurt, she retorts, and Aunt Kathi is also in favor.

When you go to kiss her at the door, she draws back.

"That reminds me!" she exclaims. "We've an appointment with the beautician next week."

"*We* have *what*?"

"You're having your blackheads removed next Wednesday. She may be able to do something about those spots too. Anyway, you're going. You look awful with that pus oozing out of your chin and nose and heaven knows where else. Fräulein Alexandra is very good at her job."

When you're fuming and don't have a safety valve, the answer is to take a cab to the Jack Point and indulge yourself.

The bag of laundry is in your way at the amusement arcade. You ask the man at the cash desk to look after it. He nods without looking up and pencils in something on his crossword puzzle.

Unimportant things work better than usual when you're feeling frustrated. You're a wizard at pinball, you beat the Serbs hands down at foosball, and you win the world soccer championship 6:1. The fiver machine swallows coin after coin. An unkempt old guy who's often there but never plays the machines, just drinks wine, takes it into his head to accost you at the counter. To make matters worse, his breath smells.

You ask him to give you a break.

You're in his regular place, he insists.

Because it isn't a good day—in fact, it's a bad one after a series of good ones with Laura—you tell him to get lost.

"Who do you think you are, fatso, a reverend?"

When you descend to arguing with someone as deranged as that, you can't get back on track yourself. For a moment you realize you're going downhill. Downhill in the world, in the society and life of your choice. One that bears little resemblance to the one you used to aspire to.

You stand up, seething. The old guy is your enemy.

He's furious. He looks like he's about to spit. But you're more furious still.

NOTE TO SELF: When two people fight, what always counts is which of them is the madder. The winner will be the one whose anger is more intense.

You take a step forward. The old guy stands his ground. The instant you draw back your fist, you feel rage coupled with profound satisfaction that you're going to lash out at last.

Anyone who gets involved in a fistfight should possess a certain basic knowledge of how to handle himself. One punch in the kisser, a thud, and your opponent goes flying? That happens only in the movies. If you don't know how to deliver a straight left to the jaw, you don't just miss. You make yourself look ridiculous for one thing; for another, the old guy catches you with a feeble roundhouse to the side of the head. You just have time to kick him in the shins before the Jack Point's bouncers rush up and separate you.

"The stoned reverend and old Boris," you hear them mutter. "Who'd have thought it?"

You feel so humiliated in your role as the stoned reverend who picked a fight with old Boris, you leave your bag of laundry behind.

Are you going to let Fräulein Alexandra loose on your face or incur Mom's wrath? Such appointments are hard to get and cost a lot. You can imagine what she'd say if you called the beauty parlor and canceled the treatment.

Besides, you want to look your best for Laura. That clinches it, so you rendezvous with Mom at the beauty parlor after all. You're introduced to the woman in charge and all her underlings. Mom is proud of being on first-name terms with the boss, just as it flatters her to be on similar terms with restaurateurs or the owners of dry cleaners. She discusses your courses and academic achievements. You stand alongside, squinting at a pair of legs protruding from a miniskirt not far off.

NOTE TO SELF: When you're squirming beneath Fräulein Alexandra's fingertips, you realize how women suffer in the cause of beauty.

"You really ought to consider doing something about your face," she says when the treatment is over and you're mopping the tears from your eyes.

"I've often thought that myself," you reply.

"I'm thinking in-depth treatment. Face lotion. Moisture cream."

"Yes? You think so?"

Because you can hardly say no, you nod as you watch Fräulein Alexandra fill a bag with exorbitantly expensive beauty preparations. She's pretty, you notice, but her smile is thoroughly businesslike.

"How would you like to pay, cash or card?"

If you're twenty-two and have to wait until your mother's treatment is over and she emerges to settle the bill, you decide it's better to refrain from flirting.

The way people live says a lot about them, and not everyone who resides in a tub is a philosopher. Since men have no eye for detail except in striptease joints, women's homes are nicer in comparison. So the first time your beloved invites you to her home you can't wait to see if she has taste.

Having gotten by for years with a mattress, a decrepit clothes closet, and a rather rickety little table, you're highly impressed to find that Laura's apartment contains furniture worthy of being called furniture. Although dark and on the damp side, it's better kept than any apartment you've seen for years. There are even houseplants. You spontaneously decide to acquire some yourself. An apartment without greenery looks lifeless.

What surprises you most of all is the drum kit in the living room. You learn that Laura has been playing the drums for seven years.

When you weigh 240 pounds and are reputed to be a stoned minister of religion, you're utterly delighted to find yourself in the company of a woman who lives in a trim apartment, can play the drums, and is three years older than yourself.

The latter fact is particularly beneficial to your image. A man in whom older women are interested must be mature and, thus, more interesting than his male contemporaries.

Laura is cooking. It's your first real evening together. You look through her record collection while she's busy in the kitchen. A lot of her records you know. Many of them you've never heard of. They include some classical music.

"Charlie, would you *please* stop singing?" Laura calls from the kitchen.

"Sorry," you call back.

"You're welcome to put some music on," she adds.

She can't see you're standing beside the record cabinet, so it's a coincidence fraught with deeper meaning. It signifies instinctive mutual understanding.

NOTE TO SELF: When you're in love you see omens everywhere.

Before serving, she asks if she can put on something other than the crap you picked out, which some crackbrain left behind.

You nod. "Carry on."

She chooses some opera. You don't know what it's about, exactly, but it's definitely opera. The sounds that fill the room are appalling, but you refuse to accept that this discrepancy in musical taste is an omen.

Even if the first meal your new girlfriend cooks for you tastes awful, you manage to relish it after the fifth or sixth mouthful.

Laura asks if you need salt or more roasted onions. She gives a lengthy account of how the dish was prepared and lectures you on the complications that arose. Meanwhile, a woman with a crystalline voice belts out an aria.

In midconversation you grasp that Laura is a veggie.

Very soon afterward, you grasp that she assumes her new boyfriend is a veggie too.

One embarks on a relationship with all kinds of hopes and dreams. Many are serious, many are lighthearted, many relate to one's career and success—for instance, when one has gotten to know some influential people—and many are centered on children and personal happiness. Most of them are dashed sooner or later, but any love is strong at first, especially one as great as you feel for Laura. Not even the shattering experience of milk pudding and bean stew with herbs can alter the fact that Laura's eyes are dark brown and glorious. Her hair speaks to you, her hands are all the solace in the world.

After a dessert so sweet your teeth itch, you retire to the bedroom, where Laura's hands cease to be all the solace in the world and become the most elementary part of your preparation for the world's true solace.

When you're lying in bed for the first time with the woman you love, everything's great. The bed is great. The view from the bed is great. The color of the parquet floor is great, the pictures on the walls are great, the drapes are great, the bookcase is great, the smell is great, even the insane music from the living room is great. You don't question whether the bed is soft. That's unimportant.

NOTE TO SELF: Lovers lose their sense of perspective.

When lying in bed with your new girlfriend, you remember the famous test devised by a German countess. You read about it in Aunt Ernestine's copy of *Woman in the Mirror*.

This test enables you to discover if you've found the right mate. You need only sniff the nape of their neck, which—claims the countess—smells of itself. If you find the smell pleasant, you'll harmonize excellently with the person of your choice. If it smells of nothing or is less than pleasant, you'll never share a park bench or feed the pigeons with that person when you're eighty. At least you'll get a definite result, or so Countess von Dannewitz swears.

When you sniff the nape of Laura's neck while she's asleep, you get a result that allows of only one conclusion: Countess von Dannewitz is crazy. You've never loved anyone the way you love Laura and you intend to love her forever. So it doesn't mean a thing that the nape of her neck smells of rancid bouillon.

Being in a relationship with a female drummer, you daydream about founding a band with her.

Lying on your bed at home and listening to "Dancing Queen," you picture yourself onstage. You're the lead singer. Thousands of hands are clapping and waving to you. Although you're the undisputed star, you point to Laura and applaud her after a drum solo. Groupies leap onto the stage and hand you slips of paper bearing their phone numbers. One girl is particularly insistent. Weeping, she says she'll kill herself if you don't give in to her. I'm sorry, you tell her. I sympathize, but I'd never cheat on Laura. Roadies drag the sobbing girl off the stage. And so on.

After the tenth hearing of "Dancing Queen" you've had enough and realize how absurd these daydreams are. You'd never dare ask Laura if you could sing. Still, being famous is a fascinating thought. It would be good enough if Laura achieved fame without a band and your participation. Generally speaking, everyone wishes their beloved were the greatest. And, generally speaking, everyone—without evil intent—does all they can to prevent that glorious development (from *The Path to Self-Awareness*).

A new relationship means new friends, new insights, new habits, new challenges.

You're introduced to Laura's best friend, Rosemarie, who has a five-month-old daughter and has been convinced, ever since attending a shamanistic seminar, that Jörg Haider is the reincarnation of Kemal Atatürk. She never looks you in the eye when you're talking to her and picks her nose when she thinks no one's looking. You're appalled by what she does with the product of her excavations.

You're invited with Laura to Arnold and Heike's. Not only are they the most assiduous pot smokers in town, but they like to document what they do in a curiously methodical way. Every detail of their highs is recorded on grubby pieces of paper. Duration, intensity, sensation. Where the high "came from," whether from below, behind, above, or the side. You've no idea what this means, but they insist you smoke with them and keep a record of your own impressions.

Arnold and Heike own a cat that displays eccentric behavior, having been driven insane by the fumes and the music played on these occasions. They don't think much of personal hygiene. In their view, showering every day is a compulsive act imposed on the individual by society.

At their home you meet Sophie, who has a pet white mouse, is proud of her nose ring, and hopes very soon to marry Nasser, her Egyptian boyfriend, and move to his native land with him. Sophie takes you off to Special Butohs, a dance theater where only leg amputees perform. You clap and pronounce their performance absolutely wonderful.

You're assigned a walk-on role in an experimental movie directed by Marco, a self-taught cineast. Clad in a loincloth, you have to stand in the middle of an intersection and repeat, over and over again: "They moved out of Paris, and no one cares a hill of beans about them anymore." This earns you a mention in the credits.

At the beginning of a relationship your beloved can serve you up any old crap and you'll say yea and amen to everything. Everything's great, including your girlfriend's friends, no matter how prickly and hard to get used to they are.

Sadly, none of Laura's friends like Karl May. They also regard being overweight as a character defect.

When you get to know Laura's friends better, you find that Marco is the most likable of them. He infects you with his enthusiasm for *Twin Peaks*, a TV series in which the members of the cast are so good-looking, you're painfully reminded of Paoletta. He suggests that everyone watch every episode as a group from now on, and you're far from averse to this idea. It's such a creepy series, you'd never dream of watching an episode on your own.

The night you happen to be hosting the *Twin Peaks* get-together, everyone says they're coming: Sophie and Nasser, Arnold and Heike with their shoebox of grass, Marco, and even Rosemarie the nose-picker, who's leaving the baby with her boyfriend for the evening.

Being about to entertain your girlfriend's friends for the first time, you pour yourself a glass with a tremulous hand several hours in advance. These people have known Laura a long time and are thoroughly acquainted with her and her past. You're the new guy in town, so it's essential to make a good impression.

You go shopping with Laura for French fries and drinks. You worry you may feel lonely among so many new friends, so you have to invite Mirko. He was originally going to look after Mimi; now he'll collect the cat and come back later as a guest. And because you want to show you also know some interesting personalities, it's not a bad idea to call the FIST chairman. If he has a spat with someone, so be it. At least it'll inject some life into the party, and you can't be held responsible for your friends' behavior.

NOTE TO SELF: If you're looking forward to a party and hope it'll go well, you may possibly convince yourself of the truth of an old saying: that more tears are shed over answered prayers than unanswered.

After *Twin Peaks* the guests push the table and chairs aside. Your bulky mattress is propped against the wall. Sophie puts on a record she's brought along, and everyone starts dancing the tango. Nearly all of them can do it too. Even the FIST chairman goes strutting across the room like a crow. You're the only person aside from Mirko who simply watches.

Someone uses the phone. You don't see who it is, but you hear the receiver being slammed down on the cradle from time to time. More guests show up at brief intervals. The door to your apartment remains permanently open. New arrivals whom you've never seen before are greeted with roars of approval. You exchange a glance with Mirko. He raises his eyebrows.

Later on there's live music as well, but you try not to lose your nerve. It's best to retreat to the bathroom and eat some chocolate.

After a while, someone knocks and the FIST chairman asks if you can spare a moment. You open the door. He slips inside and perches on the edge of the bathtub.

"Been thinking it over?"

"No, I just wanted a little peace and quiet. It's pandemonium out there."

"Bullshit! I meant my idea. You and me in Germany, coining it."

"Oh, that. Sorry, it's not my bag. Door-to-door selling? Count me out. No."

"But I've already put your name down for it. It kicks off in four weeks' time!"

"Now just a minute…"

He knocks off his cigarette ash on the edge of the bath. You heard him, he says. You've already been assigned with him—you'll make a lot of money. You've already signed on.

"I never signed a thing!"

He rises and rests a hand on your shoulder.

"Please don't stand me up. What am I supposed to do, go on my own? How would I explain your signature?"

Your head is spinning as you rejoin the revelers.

A guy with a black beard and mustache has brought his guitar along. Some maracas appear from somewhere and dulcet voices fill the air. Mirko, who has promised to stay on at your insistence, locks himself in the bathroom. Your inquisitive next-door neighbor, an accountant type who rings your doorbell at every opportunity and asks all kinds of questions, not that you've ever invited him in, is seated at the table with the others, putting away your Valpolicella. You spot a joint between his fingers. For a while, musical performances alternate with spiritualist sessions. Everyone has dilated pupils. Later, you even sight a skinhead among the guests. Laura tries to allay your not-inconsiderable anxiety by explaining that he's a harmless Redskin. He's also a pathetic soul who wants Rosemarie to exorcise him.

From time to time the FIST chairman prowls around you and pleads with you not to stand him up.

When your apartment is transformed into a madhouse under the control of psychopathic total strangers, it's time to get a grip. Although you're an 87 percent wimp, and, as such, not in favor of vehemence and harsh words, even a 3 percent adventurer encounters situations in which he finds it hard not to use expressions like "stupid, inconsiderate scumbags."

When you opt for the only practical solution, which is to call a cab at one a.m. and go to the Jack Point with Mirko, nobody notices.

When you return to the smoke-filled apartment without Mirko at three a.m., nobody notices because the atmosphere has meantime been enlivened by the spirit of a deceased Indian yogi.

The FIST chairman has disappeared. In the kitchen you discover something on your bulletin board that resembles a train timetable.

If a friend pressures you into going to Germany with him to make money, telling Mirko is the last thing you should do.

"Great idea!" he exclaims. "When are you off?"

"I'm *not*! I've no wish to go from door to door—"

"You *are*. You can't leave a friend in the lurch—that's the one thing you must never do. Leaving a friend in the lurch is a mortal sin."

You object that it's anything but an act of friendship to forge someone's signature and coerce him into a job he doesn't want to do.

"Nonsense! It won't hurt you. You'll come home with lots of moola. And experience! There's no substitute for it, buddy."

Commit one mistake and you commit another, so you ask Mom what she thinks of the idea.

"About time too! Studying at university is an unremunerative occupation. Uncle Johann agrees."

The FIST chairman calls and reminds you to bring a white gown to wear when you're going from door to door. That's so you look like a genuine medic.

"I most certainly *won't*! I'm not traipsing around dressed up like a house painter! I can't, anyway. What about Mimi?"

"Oh, forget the fucking cat! We'll be together, earning money during the day and having fun nights!"

NOTE TO SELF: When you're faced with a choice and can't decide one way or the other, the best thing is to lock yourself in and turn off the phone.

On the morning of your planned departure, someone hammers on the front door so loudly, you go and open it, all naked and flabby. Only then do you draw breath and think, but by then it's too late.

Mirko squeezes past you into the apartment and proceeds to pack a suitcase and a traveling bag. The FIST chairman looks at you appealingly. Downstairs, Laura is waiting to drive you to the station and take care of the cat in your absence.

Standing transfixed in the doorway, you only register passing neighbors, their good mornings and astonished expressions, through a kind of mist. Articles of clothing are hurled at you. It takes you a while to absorb Mirko's order to put them on—and his query as to the whereabouts of your passport. Your *passport*, man!

On the journey to Stuttgart the FIST chairman plies you with beer and schnapps and tries to liven things up with the aid of his pocket radio. He paints the next few weeks in the rosiest colors and promises you won't regret this. There'll be lots of pretty girls.

"When you're on your way from one door to the next, don't you think you'll sometimes come across a lonely heart?"

"You mean you…"

"You bet! There was this blonde with boobs like…"

Unobtrusively, you deposit Nietzsche's *Zarathustra* on the fold-down table between you, but he doesn't seem interested. You pick up the book and make like you want to read it, but he doesn't care. All he's thinking about is women. He tops up your glass of schnapps.

You're drunk by the time you get to the German frontier. So is the FIST chairman, and the blonde's boobs are even bigger. Just after Passau the blonde becomes a brunette. In the vicinity of Nuremberg the FIST chairman regularly spent the night with said brunette. Outside Stuttgart the brunette had a sister with whom he also went to bed, but in Stuttgart itself, immediately after reporting to the firm that recruited you, you're informed that your pitch is in the Mannheim area, whereas the FIST chairman is being sent off to Bremerhaven.

NOTE TO SELF: Circumstances defy your comprehension when you're drunk.

"Out of the question!" yells the FIST chairman. He thumps the desk so hard, the papers on it flutter in all directions. "Herr Kolostrum and I are a team, that was the arrangement!"

More men in suits and colored neckties converge from adjacent offices, he bellows so loudly.

"You don't understand," says the departmental chief. "We've no place for the two of you together. This is the way you've been assigned and this is how you'll operate, one here and the other there. You can manage without each other for a few weeks. Absence makes the heart grow fonder!"

He makes kissing sounds and winks.

If a friend is your only real reason for going someplace and that friend is suddenly snatched away, you're in the depths of despair. Especially if the name of the place is Stuttgart.

If you weren't an 87 percent wimp and a 3 percent adventurer, but the other way around, you could bid the FIST chairman an immediate farewell, tear up the contract bearing the forged signature, and go back home. But because you're an 82 percent conformist, your team leader welcomes you to the Mannheim area late that evening.

Your team consists of eight young men who give you a reasonably friendly reception. The rules are explained right away. You live together, eat together, belong together. The household chores are shared. The cook's name is Günther. You wash up your own things. During the day, each man patrols his own route.

You receive your instructions the same night. The recommended standard intro is: "Good morning/afternoon, Herr/Frau Doorbell, my name is such and such, and I'm from the Red Cross in so-and-so. Don't worry, there's nothing wrong. It's about a donation." Winning smile.

If the door isn't slammed in your face, you have to extract a signature from the person in question. This gives the Red Cross authorized access to the donor's bank account and enables it to debit a fixed annual contribution. Of this amount the canvasser gets 300 percent and the firm 50 percent. This means it'll be three-and-a-half years before the Red Cross benefits from the donor's nobility of mind. Team leader Klaus gives an arithmetical example that makes it clear what a gold mine you've stumbled on. If someone donates DM10 per month, or DM120 per annum, the canvasser gets DM360.

Jesus, you think, as much as that! You retire to bed rubbing your hands.

The next day you begin by going around with the team leader to see how he softens people up. Then you're allowed to take off on your own.

At ten in the morning, suffering from a headache and heartburn, you ring a Frau Butterweck's doorbell. And are admitted.

By one p.m. precisely you've chalked up DM50.

You decide not to brave the November cold any longer. In the only pizzeria in town you devour a plateful of lasagne. You're the only customer. You order yourself another plateful. And after that a tiramisu. At two you return to the fray. Discounting three cigarette breaks, you work through until seven. You sign up one donor after another without really grasping why people are so generous.

NOTE TO SELF: If you're feeling happy, just wait. There's bound to be a downside.

Late that afternoon you ring the doorbell of the Sonderstuhl house. The door is opened by a girl, presumably the daughter of the house. She stares at you, bursts out laughing, and calls over her shoulder:

"Hey, come and look at the Michelin man!"

When you're on your own in a strange town and someone insults you, you find a quiet corner and shed a tear or two.

At half past seven you rendezvous with the others outside the church. Klaus has scored DM150, Günther DM120, the rest between DM50 and DM100. Your own haul amounts to DM130.

The others glower and avoid your eye, but Klaus pats you on the back and beams at you. As team leader he gets 5 percent of every donation you chalk up.

It's always interesting to meet people who have undergone widely varying experiences in life. What matters, however, is the context in which these encounters take place. It's one thing to carry on a conversation in a bar with cosmopolitan characters like American students or Japanese action painters. It's another to sit in an unheated communal kitchen in the German boondocks, listening to the savage vituperations hurled at God and the world in general by loutish and obviously paranoid table companions who strive to outdo one another in volume and extremism. When you sit at supper with a bunch of such individuals, you hear some remarkable things.

Fritz from Kufstein is a convicted rapist. Klaus learned this by accident. Fritz begs the team leader not to tell anyone or he'll be fired. Klaus says he'll think about it.

Günther, a socially dysfunctional trucker with a strong propensity for physical violence, believes that van Gogh is a midfield player for Feyenoord Rotterdam, and only a psychological dunce would take it into his head to correct this minor misapprehension.

Norbert, who's studying electrical engineering in Graz, trades in porn magazines, Hungarian cigarettes, hooch, and German phone cards, which he obtains from God knows where and sells to his teammates at half price.

The team leader appears to be most rational of the lot. Although Klaus sometimes peps everyone up and provides one or other member of team with moral support, he privately seems to keep his distance from the group.

They're all unlikable.

Most of them are scared of Günther, you notice that at supper. No one ever contradicts him. Günther's attitude toward Klaus, on the other hand, is one of doglike devotion. He beams like a little boy at any word of praise from the team leader and harps on his ambitions to become Klaus's deputy. He's as thick as two short planks. The most he ever had to do with a university was painting some classrooms. He resembles a brutal member of a street gang, and Klaus acts like his probation officer. Günther's spaghetti isn't al dente, it's mush. No one complains, though.

What's more, there's far too little of it.

After supper you're asked for DM50, your contribution to the household expenses. Then you're privileged to wash up with Fritz. Meantime, the day's returns are analyzed. The team leader writes down some figures. You go to bed but can't sleep for the dirty jokes emanating from the beds around you. You wonder how Laura is.

When you're lying on a creaking cot surrounded by mentally and spiritually deranged individuals, hungry but without even a candy bar to console you, you yearn for Mimi's soft fur. For the smell of your own apartment. For Wild West novels. For cafés. Even for the FIST chairman. This brings you to the helpful conclusion that what you previously considered a sorry existence was really a thing of beauty.

Just before you fall asleep, images of the real world flash into your head and you see Paoletta in front of you.

On your second day you chalk up another DM130. That night, when you stretch out on your cot, it collapses to the delight of your teammates. You spend that and subsequent nights sleeping on the floor.

On the third day you score DM120, on the fourth DM140. It's seldom that any of the others collect more than you. Only the team leader achieves DM200 or more. None of this helps, though. You long to go home.

On the afternoon of the fifth day you have a remarkable experience. You ring at a door and a skinhead opens it. Beyond him you glimpse more shaven heads. The gentlemen are playing cards and drinking. Music is blaring.

Panic-stricken, you reel off your spiel like a tape recorder. You're expecting to be thumped any moment.

The drinkers loudly demand to know who's there. Just a medic, the skinhead calls back.

"Come in, youngster. Like a beer?"

You're afraid you're on duty, you reply with a forced smile. "I know I can count on your generosity," you add.

He slaps you on the shoulder. "Thanks all the same, pal, but you aren't getting any bread."

Holy smoke, you say to yourself when you're back outside. The fifth day nets you DM150.

The next day Klaus comes with you. He wants to see how you operate. You go from door to door and recite your spiel. Nearly everyone asks you in.

"Now I know what does it."

You look at Klaus expectantly.

"Positive energy. Your delivery's lousy—I've never heard worse. You reel off your intro like you're about to fall asleep at any moment, but you're the best-natured guy who's ever worked this patch. People can sense that. You're no threat to them. They take to you."

On the morning of the seventh day you come to an old woman who lives in a shabbily furnished apartment reeking of mildew and rancid cooking oil. You're on the point of backing out—there's nothing doing here—but the old woman restrains you. She wants to make a donation. You're ushered into the living room.

"Wait here!"

She returns from the kitchen laden with tea and pastries.

"You sing very nicely, young man. Sing me something."

Unaware that you were singing, you blush and shyly say you'd rather not. She smiles. Then she tries to give you a five-mark coin. Where's your collecting box?

You explain that collecting boxes are out these days. People donate via their bank accounts.

She thinks for a moment. Then she says she gets a pension of DM1000 a month. She'd like to donate a hundred of that. The Red Cross replaced her hip and she wants to express her gratitude.

You ask if she really wants to donate DM1200 a year.

She wants to donate DM100 a month, she replies.

"But DM100 a month makes DM1200 a year, Frau Enders."

"Yes! That's what I want to donate! Have a pastry, young man."

The pastries have mold on them.

"Frau Enders, DM1200 a year is a lot of money. Sure you want to donate so much?"

"Quite sure."

You think of all the people you've come across in the last few days. The families with meager or modest incomes who readily donate. The rich folk who threaten you with the cops over the intercom unless you beat it at once. The intimidating barking of dogs from inside suburban villas. And now you're sitting with a little old woman on a tiny pension whose donation means DM3600 for the canvasser.

When you don't know what to say in such a situation, it's best to let the old woman talk. She's happy to have a listener. You ask how her hip is doing, inquire after her children and grandchildren. Then you stand up, say you don't have the requisite paperwork with you, and bow out.

"Such a nice young man," you hear her say on the stairs before she shuts her door.

Although it's only eleven, you decide to take a break. You go looking for an inn. They're all closed. Not a single one opens in the morning in the dump where Klaus dropped you. He probably had his reasons.

It's icy cold. The place is shrouded in mist. An occasional car drives past. A small delivery van, a truck. Pedestrians are a rare sight.

You grab a chance to warm up for a while in a bakery. It smells divine in there. Common to all Central European countries, the scent of bread, cakes, and pastries makes you feel homesick. To allay your emotional turmoil, you think it best to buy a few rolls and recall what John Wayne tells his son in a Western: "When you come back, you'll be a man."

There are seven hours to go before your rendezvous, so you tell John Wayne to stuff it and don't ring any more door-bells. You lean against a wall. Smoke. Tour the district to see if any of those goddamned inns have opened yet. The time drags by agonizingly slowly.

This is the Apocalypse, you think. It certainly looks that way. Everything is gray. Cold. Not a soul on the streets. Not an inn open. The few people around are outcasts. Mailmen. Hucksters. Flier distributors. Pizza deliverymen. Nothing happens. Nothing.

That evening you get into Klaus's car frozen stiff.

"Well, how much?" he asks, eyes shining.

You shake your head.

"You don't say! I bet Günther you'd break the two-hundred barrier today."

"I'm going home."

"I guessed as much," says the team leader.

NOTE TO SELF: If you're only a 10 percent shoulder-shrugger you aren't tough enough to earn your money properly.

You're so glad to get back from door-to-door selling in Germany, nothing else seems even half as tragic. You have a wonderful time with Laura. You're happy. You've enough cash to last you several months and a lot can happen in that time, so you don't worry. The world is tough, but it's a great place. No more dark thoughts can assail you now.

You're undaunted even by the prospect of the family festivities at Christmas. If you have to pull your socks up for a couple hours and sing the eternal songs of Christendom, so what? But you'll have to get your hair cut first.

NOTE TO SELF: Everyone should have a hairdresser who knows them.

When you go to the hairdresser shortly before Christmas, you're attended to by an imperious blonde who owns the business and is riled by the turmoil that precedes the holiday season. She doesn't listen when you tell her how you want your hair cut. She barks at her trainees left and right. Then she moistens your hair with an atomizer and proceeds to snip away.

It's nice at the hairdresser's when you shut your eyes, relax, and have your hair gently shorn.

It's not so nice when the hairdresser periodically interrupts your contemplative interlude by yelling like a drill sergeant.

It's even less nice when, after the woman announces that she's through, you open your eyes and see an extremely ugly stranger in the mirror.

She roughly brushes the snippings off your face and neck. At the cash desk she demands an unexpectedly large sum. You still can't steel yourself to say anything about your terrible haircut.

It's too late once you've paid. Although you grossly overtip the woman, she disappears into the back room without a word. You stand there, staring at the charity piggy bank beside the till. You don't dare take another look in the mirror.

Back home you inspect the disaster. It looks like the hairdresser stuck a pudding basin on your head and cut around the rim. You can't be seen anywhere like that. You wrestle with yourself. How is an 82 percent conformist to go back to a hairdressing salon and complain that he's had an unacceptable haircut?

Maybe charm and amiability will do it.

Back at the salon you ask to speak with the boss. After a while she comes slouching out with a sullen air. She neither recognizes nor remembers you. With a smile, you say there's been a minor mistake. You didn't ask for a haircut like this.

"What's your problem?" she demands, loudly enough to make other customers turn around. "Everything's fine! What am I supposed to have done, cut your hair *badly*?"

You indicate what you mean with your hands and mumble that you didn't mean it that way. She seizes you roughly by the head and plucks at random tufts of hair.

"That's okay, nothing to complain of there. The next time, express yourself more clearly. Simply say what you want. Exactly what don't you like?"

Meantime, all present are staring at you. You're feeling in the wrong. Relieved, you agree with her when she demonstrates that there's nothing wrong with your haircut. You nod, thank her effusively, and hit your head on the door, which is shut, because you're in such a hurry to get out of there.

Back in front of the mirror at home, you're so desperate you burst into tears. Christmas Eve is in three days' time. What are you going to do?

On closer inspection, you think you've identified the biggest problem areas. Resolutely, you pick up the scissors. A snip here, a snip there, another here, another there. The result isn't wholly satisfactory. You start sweating. You have to cut off some more in one or two places. You continue to snip and snip away.

NOTE TO SELF: *When you cut your own hair in front of the mirror, you very soon resemble a psychiatric patient after a fit.*

Having drunk a coffee and recovered from the shock, you go to another hairdresser and get him to shave your head. Some left-wing students jeer you on the way home. You walk faster, in a crouch. Yells can be heard behind you. You're pelted with snowballs from every direction. There's a thud, and you get the feeling that the snowball that hit you on the head must have had a stone embedded in it. Clutching your flabby stomach, you break into a run.

Cries of horror and disapproval greet you when you show up bald for the family get-together on Christmas Eve, and you're scolded all evening. You can't imagine what Aunt Ernestine will say about your new haircut, so you visit her on Christmas Day wearing a cap and refuse to take it off on the grounds you're suffering from a skin disease. Sympathetically, Aunt Ernestine gives you one more bill than she did last year. She talks about the rising crime rate.

You hardly recognize her. She looks pale and has lost weight, but her calves are twice their usual size. They're edematous. You quickly look away.

NOTE TO SELF: Baldness is considered attractive in older men only.

You come from a family in which superstitions, premonitions, and other occultisms are rife. That's why, fuddled with sleep, you pull on your clothes during the night of December 25–26 after once more dreaming that Aunt Ernestine has been taken ill.

You have such violent palpitations, you're afraid of falling over. Gritting your teeth, you stagger into the bathroom and splash your face with cold water. You take the spare keys to Aunt Ernestine's from the hook. You check the time while waiting for someone at the cab company to answer the phone. Three thirty a.m.

It's snowed a little, and the taxi skids around the bends. The Turkish driver laughs at this. He's eager to engage his fare in conversation. Unfortunately, his German is poor. You nod at him for courtesy's sake, no matter what he says. You catch odd words only: "Schnapps…shift…schnapps…spiced buns… Mustapha…Monday…" And again and again: "Hauspeter, Hauspeter!" He gets more and more worked up. Sometimes he grins, sometimes he angrily slaps the steering wheel, mutters something, and says *Inshallah!* A moment later he's laughing again.

You smile at him. You find the situation unpleasant, but you don't know what to do. Sitting back in silence, you watch the man becoming more and more heated. You'd like to get out, but the driver might be offended and you don't want to run the risk.

He laughs uproariously. "Hauspeter, Hauspeter!" he cries again, and uses both hands to demonstrate how he would strangle someone. The wheel spins, the cab performs a pirouette just as you're crossing a big square. Luckily, there's no other car in the vicinity. The driver manages to regain control. This incident energizes him still more. Smiling all over his face and bouncing around in his seat, he yells, "Hauspeter, Hauspeterrr!"

Back rammed into the upholstery and fingers clutching the grab handle, you pray you'll reach your destination without any more serious incident. You've long felt uneasy about the driver, but where are you going to find the missing 90-odd percent of an adventurer you need to ask him to let you out? You can only try to pacify him.

"Are you talking about someone named Hans-Peter, driver?" you inquire politely.

The driver gives a start and turns around, leaving the steering wheel to its own devices.

"You know? You know Hauspeter?"

You gather from the driver's incoherent blather that he suspects you of being a good friend of one Hans-Peter, on whom he has sworn to take revenge. With one hand on the door handle, ready to jump out onto the asphalt, you assure him you've never crossed the path of anyone by that name. The driver eventually accepts this. He laughs and reprises the act of strangulation.

NOTE TO SELF: *When being driven by a demented cabby, take care what you say.*

Having reached Aunt Ernestine's unscathed and handed over an enormous tip, you pace up and down for a while. You can't wait to go inside and take a look, but the cabby's driving style has left you feeling nauseous.

You scrape some snow off the yard fence and rub it over your face. You look up at the windows. Not a light on anywhere. Not a sound to be heard in the vicinity. Even the sound of the departing cab has died away long ago.

You listen at the front door before turning the key. Nothing. You heart speeds up again. Is Aunt Ernestine still alive?

You bite your lip, the door to the apartment creaks so loudly. Tentatively, you close it behind you. You remain motionless for several minutes so as not to make a noise and allow your eyes to get used to the darkness. Over there, just down the hall, Aunt Ernestine is lying in bed. You can hear no snoring, no breathing, nothing, and it's pitch-dark.

When you're fat and need to move silently, the answer is to distribute your weight.

The floorboards creak at every step you take. And so, after minutes of indecision, you do what you've done on nearly all your nocturnal visits: you lie down on the floor and crawl toward Aunt Ernestine's bed to satisfy yourself that she's still alive. With a stifled groan you kneel down, supporting yourself on your hands, and stretch out on your stomach.

A fraction of a second later you're back on your feet and yelling with all your might.

"Ouch! Right in the guts! Ouch, ouch, ouch!"

Instinctively you grope for the light switch and turn it on. In the dull glow of a standard lamp you see that your stomach is peppered with thumbtacks. Looking down, you discover that Aunt Ernestine—probably for fear of burglars—has strewn them all over the floor.

Roused by the clamor, Aunt Ernestine sits up in bed with a start and sees a fat, bald-headed stranger hopping around the room and uttering cries of anguish.

NOTE TO SELF: Some human hearts last the course for a hundred years, but excitement can prove too much for them after that.

There's no autopsy when an old woman dies because everyone's delighted that there's one less burden on the public purse.

You don't want to go to prison, so you refrain from telling anyone about your last visit to Aunt Ernestine. For some days you walk around in circles suffering from pangs of conscience. Tears alternate with apologies addressed to thin air. You find it hard to endure, being unable to share your guilty secret with anyone.

In this state of mind you're coerced by Aunt Kathi into attending the reading of Ernestine's will. Though unsurprised to learn that she's left you the bulk of her money, you're staggered to discover that she blew nearly all of it during her lifetime. The house didn't belong to her; she had right of residence only. There are a mere hundred thousand schillings left in the bank, and of this she wanted you to have half.

NOTE TO SELF: Even piddling sums of money can give rise to testamentary disputes.

You hear little about the vendettas that break out because, with a heavy heart, you spend weeks closeted within your own four walls and don't even visit Mom for clean laundry purposes. What's certain is that you won't see anything of your legacy for a long time because various distant relations are laying claim to your fifty thousand schillings and Aunt Kathi has set her lawyers on them. You don't want the money anyway, so you hardly listen to her telephone reports of these goings-on.

When a family member dies, you wonder if they can read your mind in the afterlife—if they're keeping you under surveillance.

Thoughts of this kind haunt you at the most inappropriate moments. Aunt Ernestine pops into your head while you're jerking off on the bed. Is she watching? Is she saying to herself, "My God, what's that in the boy's hand?"

If you become obsessed with such considerations, they can render you incapable of jerking off for weeks on end, let alone having sex with your girlfriend.

You pick up a porn magazine: Can Aunt Ernestine see you? You're having a bath: Is Aunt Ernestine watching? You stuff yourself with candy bars: Does Aunt Ernestine disapprove? You're thinking ill of other people: Is Aunt Ernestine listening?

NOTE TO SELF: When relations die, you can't shake off the suspicion that their souls are drifting through your home like an invisible mist.

The nights are worst of all. A bad dream jolts you awake. At first you don't know where you are. Then you think of Aunt Ernestine and believe you can sense her presence. You sometimes wonder if she's forgiven you or if she and the Bonesetter are plotting together.

It's unpleasant, the thought that you're being persecuted from the hereafter.

You can't continue to afford the apartment without Aunt
Ernestine's financial contributions, and Laura is too independent to ever move in with a boyfriend. Because you're
afraid of ghosts on your own at night, you take a cheap room
in a shared apartment where there's a washing machine and
Mimi is welcome. Your fellow residents are Inge and "Red"
Walter.

Walter is so called because he's a promising member of
the Young Socialists. He weighs two hundred pounds, sports
a beard and mustache, wears pebble glasses, and likes classical
music. When drunk he listens to dreary string quartets and
abandons himself to *Weltschmerz*. You've never met a man
who's always so close to tears, but you'd never know it during
the day.

Inge comes from Carinthia, is studying business admin-
istration, and weighs ninety pounds. It's her habit to make
general inferences from physical characteristics. You're confronted by this interpretative obsession in the first few days.
She catches sight of your hairless chest in the bathroom.
Indicating it with an outstretched forefinger, she says curtly,
"Heart attack candidate." Dismayed, you ask what she means.

Inge explains that a hairless chest is indicative of a cardiac defect and advises you to have an annual checkup.

The apartment is in an appalling condition.

Because all three occupants are mature and conscientious individuals, they unanimously reject the idea of rotating the household chores. And because there isn't any schedule for doing the household chores, the apartment resembles a hostel for dropouts on welfare. Walter indulges in his nightly cooking orgies without restraint, and when you shuffle into the communal kitchen in the morning, rubbing your eyes, you nearly have apoplexy because he was feeling too sad to wash up.

You don't clear up after him but leave the mess as it is. Inge wouldn't dream of lifting a finger for Walter either, and since he manages to rouse himself sufficiently to scrub out the saucepans encrusted with old spaghetti and Bolognese sauce only once a week at most, the kitchen is usually a humid jungle in which the sunlight is obscured by plump bluebottles and around ten million flies.

Walter also refuses to clean the shower on the grounds that he hardly ever uses it. He has a point there.

Inge isn't always easy to live with either. She's a likable person, discounting her fantasies about physical symptoms. Regrettably, however, she suffers from sexual instability and has a weakness for hairy long-distance truckers. On mornings when the kitchen is habitable for a change, you have to be prepared to encounter one such person at the breakfast table. And the sight of a shaggy-chested long-distance trucker in his underpants—one who, even though he hails from Styria, Tirol, or Carinthia, has only the most rudimentary grasp of

German—isn't to everyone's taste, especially first thing in the morning.

Inge tells you in confidence that she likes sleeping with that kind of man. She's positively addicted to them, she says, and after all, she doesn't complain about Walter smoking or you playing loud music all day long and "singing"—she mimes the inverted commas—on the toilet, under the shower, or in the kitchen.

NOTE TO SELF: It makes up for a few things if your fellow residents are cat lovers.

Walter and Inge have tacitly assumed complete responsibility for your cat. They buy her food and litter, bring home tidbits, clean out her tray, take the spoiled creature to the vet, administer worming pills, stroke her, and allow her absolute freedom. Mimi sharpens her claws on Inge's sofa. Mimi pisses in Inge's bed. Mimi craps in Walter's shoes. Mimi smashes Inge's favorite vase. Never a harsh word.

People who are good to animals can't be all bad. Their foibles should therefore be overlooked—as long as they remain within bounds.

Your favorite radio program is *Talk Radio*, which airs at midnight every Saturday. The presenter is Dieter Moor, who's much admired for his quick wit. *Talk Radio* is a great program. You can call Dieter and discuss any subject you like as long as it's one that interests him. If he doesn't take to a caller he hangs up.

Walter is alone in having certain reservations about Dieter Moor. He considers him politically naive, but even he makes strenuous efforts to speak with him on Saturday nights. Although Inge doesn't find Dieter as enticing as her long-distance truckers, she's attracted by the thought of addressing Austria live on the radio. She'd like to send greetings to her Karls and Huberts in their cabs, but Dieter isn't too fond of that sort of thing. His is a talk show, he says, not a telephone exchange or a request program.

Secretly, you regard Dieter Moor as the epitome of intellectual brilliance and would like to discuss some weighty topics with him.

If, just for once, the broadcasting authorities manage to produce an exceptional program on radio or television, word soon gets around. Before long, ten or fifteen people are sitting in the kitchen on Saturday nights. There's a blank cassette ready and waiting in the tape recorder next door because no one wants the minutes they spend in conversation with Dieter Moor and Austria to vanish into thin air.

The program lasts two hours. Two hours in which everyone competes for the phone.

Walter is the first to hear, instead of the engaged tone, a voice informing him that he'll be put through next.

"I'm on, I'm on!" he shouts.

His face reflects his excitement. He listens. His ears turn red. He swallows hard, lights a cigarette, and takes a swig of red wine, spilling some of it over his chin. He mops himself with his shirtsleeve.

To avoid feedback, you retire to the room next door with the others and turn on the tape recorder. Everyone's yelling. They break into encouraging chants like football fans. Then the current caller is sent packing and they all fall silent.

"*Talk Radio*, hello."

"It's me, Walter."

Sniffing sounds.

"Well, Walter, what do you want to say to us?"

"Dieter, don't you agree that the Left needs reorganizing? Right-wingers are crawling out of the woodwork everywhere. My question is, don't we have any plans to combat this development? Are we all..."

A crash.

"Shit! Fuck it! That was the cat!"

Click.

Universal disappointment. Boos ring out. Worried about Mimi, you hurry into the kitchen.

Walter is sitting in the corner, a picture of misery. Mimi was playing with the tablecloth and upset a glass. Walter made an instinctive grab for it and knocked over the pitcher, which fell to the floor and smashed.

Inge proceeds to clean up. Walter swears at Dieter Moor for being so impatient. You console him, then look around for the phone. It's already in use. Laura wants to talk with Dieter Moor about love.

She fails to get through. After fifteen minutes her turn is up and Inge can have a go. She has more luck. She sends her love to Helmut, who paid her a visit last week and is now in his truck somewhere between Munich and Belgrade, then promptly hangs up. Dieter Moor is pissed. Laughter and applause. Everyone ups their alcohol intake.

You sit back and picture yourself speaking with Dieter Moor man-to-man. You've been invited to participate in his program because you know more about music than anyone else. You talk about rock and pop and callers are allowed to ask questions. Dieter Moor esteems it an honor that you accepted his invitation. After the broadcast he invites you to have a drink with him. Rather offhandedly, you accept. You accompany him to his home, where several other well-known, interesting people are waiting. You shake them all by the hand…

Walter asks you to fetch another two magnums of wine from the bar downstairs. You don't feel like it, but rather than argue you slip on your moccasins and set off.

NOTE TO SELF: *Anyone returning to a party after being away, even for a short time, feels he's missed out on something of vital importance.*

M irko's wealthy father is sick of his son's escapades, so he stops his allowance. Mirko promptly decides to attend an introductory evening for would-be taxi drivers.

"Why should *I* go?" you protest.

"Why should I go on my own?"

"But *you're* the one who wants to become a cabby!"

"You do *too*," he says firmly.

A 56 percent trickster is incapable of refusing a friend, so you accompany Mirko to the introductory evening. You read a comic book under the desk while Mirko takes notes. Toward the end, application forms are handed around. You pass yours on unread. Mirko fills out all the boxes. Not until afterward is he gracious enough to confide, over a beer at the Priamus, that he won't be attending the course on his own.

"Your signature isn't hard to forge," he says with a laugh.

NOTE TO SELF: Doctors write the way they do to prevent forged prescriptions from turning up all over the place.

Needless to say, you've no intention of attending the course. It lasts six weeks, and you've better things to do than memorize street names in stuffy lecture rooms. Well, actually you've nothing better to do, but you don't feel like working.

On the first day of the course Mirko rings your bell and bullies you into coming with him.

The same thing happens on the second day of the course.

The same thing happens on the third day of the course.

The same thing happens throughout the course.

These are weeks of agonizing suspense. You don't, of course, study for your cab driver's test, nor for your university exams. Aunt Kathi's phone calls grow more and more irate. You drink beer in the afternoon and spend as much time as you can with Laura. You have to help move her furniture around in accordance with the recommendations of a dowser who ascertained that she's sleeping above an underground watercourse.

When she's working at the Café Schiller you sit in the Priamus or pay a visit to the Jack Point. On some of these expeditions you dispense with a cab and travel by bus like everyone else. Your black hat has been permanently banished to the clothes closet. If anyone wants it, you'll make him a present of it. You never want to be the Reverend again.

NOTE TO SELF: One interesting aspect of life is that people develop and modify their opinions without ever consciously thinking about it.

When Red Walter acquires a computer, the Jack Point loses an important regular customer.

Donations from political kindred spirits have enabled Walter to buy an IBM 286. This is now installed in his room and proudly shown off to every visitor, its intended purpose being to facilitate the composition of manifestos, solidarity speeches, and punchy political slogans. Infinitely more fascinating to the owner and his fellow residents, however, is another of the machine's potential uses: gaming.

On offer are sword fights, football, shooting down UFOs, conjuring tricks, Tetris, custard-pie battles, Minesweeper, karate, pinball, card games, board games.

It's a really fine thing.

Not long after Red Walter acquires the computer, calls flood in from high schools and sundry political youth organizations wondering where his urgently needed ideas have gotten to. Since Red Walter is busy playing Napoleon capturing Moscow, you have to demonstrate your talent for telephonic storytelling. You fantasize about deceased aunts, boils on the buttocks, influenza, toothache, sciatica—even visits from the police. The latter eventuality, being the most improbable, is most readily believed.

In return for your help you're permitted to have a go at the computer. Meantime, Walter assumes responsibility for the other gamers' physical welfare. He mashes up some leftover vegetables, heats the resulting mush, and brazenly serves it up as Cuban vegetable stew. Seated at the computer, you wait for this dish to be ready.

You suddenly think of Aunt Ernestine. Tears well up in your eyes, as they do quite often. All at once, to your profound sorrow, her image appears before your mind's eye. This can happen when a person has died. It isn't essential for one to have been responsible for their death.

You hope Walter will be busy for a while yet.

When someone wants to get back to a computer game, preparing a Cuban vegetable stew takes him a mere eight minutes.

"You can't tell the size of a man's thing from his nose," says Inge. "That's a fallacy. You can tell it from his hands."

"Maybe so," you reply as you unpack the shopping bags.

She bites into an apple as red as her cheeks. Her eyes twinkle. "Show me your hands."

You sigh and go on unpacking.

"Average size is okay. Better than small. I'll let you into a secret: it doesn't have to be big, just hardworking."

Inge, who has just spent two energetic days with a guy from Styria, seems intent on continuing this penis discussion. You ask if she remembered to get the potatoes and remind her that Laura is a vegetarian. You always have to cook Laura a meal of her own.

Inge hits her forehead. She licks her fingers and sets off for the supermarket again. You breathe a sigh of relief and start improvising to the tune of "My Sweet Lord."

I'm so butch
Oh, I'm so bu-utch
Yes, I'm so butch

Everybody loves me
Yes, everybody loves me
Yes, everybody loves me
'Cos I'm so bu-utch…

Walter sticks his head into the kitchen. "Going to stop that any time soon?" he demands.

You've long had a deplorable reputation as a host. Mirko claims it's rude to serve your guests canned goulash or deep-frozen pizzas. You're a barbarian in need of refinement, he says. I simply can't cook, you reply, so he browbeats you into taking some cookery lessons from him.

The cookery lessons take place, not at Mirko's pad, but on Saturdays in the apartment you share with Inge and Walter. The advantage of this is that, when lessons are over, they can develop into impromptu parties culminating in phone calls to Dieter Moor.

Word of Mirko's teaching skills soon gets around. So does word of the convivial atmosphere that prevails at these nocturnal get-togethers. Before long, you have to put up an extra table in the spacious kitchen on Saturday nights. Since Laura has no inhibitions about bringing friends along without warning, you invite Boban as well. He's one of the movie intellectuals you meet at the bar in the art-house movie theater.

You've never met anyone like him before. He's older than you, around forty, and overweight. He has a loud, orotund way of speaking. His most noticeable feature is the paralysis that affects one side of his face. Talking with him is fun. His general knowledge is impressive and he has an opinion on everything. He earns his living as an automobile dealer.

In addition to Boban, two of Walter's socialist friends have been invited. After doing the shopping Inge retired to her room to celebrate a noisy reunion with her Styrian trucker, whose dialect is incomprehensible to everyone but her. She now ventures into the kitchen with him. Laura turns up with Sophie. They both smell of wine and are in a strident mood.

At half past eight the beef and orange ragout and Laura's potato cake are sizzling in the oven. When you take off your apron—a gift from Mirko, and adorned with obscene motifs— you're glad to be able to raise a glass yourself.

NOTE TO SELF: Life lands you in situations you hadn't reckoned with and are intellectually and emotionally overtaxed by.

When, after a spell of concentrated cooking under Mirko's direction, you turn around and are confronted by a bunch of drunks, it's an unpleasant surprise because you aren't in the same state and find it hard to join in the conversation. However, this can be remedied by consuming several glasses of wine.

But when the party includes your own girlfriend, who's sitting on Boban's lap and necking with him, an activity which the rest of those present clearly consider unexceptional, you reach the limits of your endurance.

Not knowing how to react, you sit down, pour yourself a glass of wine, and say nothing.

You're still collecting your thoughts when Boban and Sophie get into an argument. He says she's crazy to marry her Muslim boyfriend and go off to Egypt with him. Here Nasser treats her with Western permissiveness, says Boban; down there she'll be in for a rude awakening. Heated remarks fly back and forth. Laura, still sitting on another man's lap, stares out the window as if the whole thing had nothing to do with her. This difference of opinion holds little interest for you under present circumstances, so you push your chair back and continue drinking on your own beside the fridge.

To retreat to the room next door would have been the reaction of an immature youth seeking consolation from his mother. To have remained sitting at the table, on the other hand, would have meant making a total asshole of yourself.

By demonstrating disapproval of your girlfriend's behavior in this way, you gain a certain amount of sympathy from the other guests. No one comments aloud on what's going at the table, but in your corner you keep getting spoken to by people fetching wine or mineral water from the fridge.

"Where did you dig him up?" asks Walter.

"Does Boban have a problem with women?" whispers Sophie.

"If you don't do something soon," says Inge, "I'll deal with the stinker myself. And your girlfriend too. Incidentally, have you seen the size of his hands? Talk about dinner plates!"

"Ho, ho, ho, ho!" says the trucker from East Styria, waving his arms around.

When you're publicly humiliated by your girlfriend and are 97 percent short of being an adventurer, you don't know how to defend yourself. Besides, you'd sooner not be an adventurer anyway, you'd only get thumped. And if you balked—if you openly displayed your jealousy—you'd only make yourself look ridiculous. That would be the worst thing of all. Suddenly, Aunt Ernestine comes to mind. You have to stop yourself from bursting into tears.

NOTE TO SELF: When you're being treated badly, you wonder if the dearly departed are looking down from heaven and castigating your abuser.

The roast beef and orange is giving off its sweet-and-sour aroma. You dash to the stove, pull out the baking tray, and shovel helpings onto plates. Laura gets her potato cake, which she shares with Sophie. Boban and Laura aren't in a clinch any longer. It's all very confusing, and you wonder if you've witnessed a scene whose sole purpose was to coax you out of your shell. Movies are discussed until it's time for *Talk Radio*.

Sophie gets through. She tells of her love for Nasser. Thickly, she complains about Boban's prediction that Nasser will mutate into a fundamentalist "down there."

"What an idiot," says Dieter Moor.

Not being adept at resolving relationship issues and conducting distasteful conversations, you hesitate to have it out with Laura. You're scared of the answers you might get. And because she's gentler to you in the next few days and refrains from broaching the subject, you tend to regard the incident as a unique aberration occasioned by overindulgence in alcohol—one that she herself has regretted ever since.

Lying in bed with some music blaring, you picture yourself dealing with Boban. Two or three elegant punches are enough to floor him. He lies twitching on a stretch of poop-infested grass. Paoletta and other spectators are standing around, whispering together. Laura bites her lip. When she sees you being besieged by other women, she hurries over. You get into the papers because Boban turns out to be a wanted criminal. A TV station calls...

After you've restored your self-respect by mowing down some Vietcong with Walter, Mirko smilingly escorts you to the examination for cab drivers. He thinks he can coerce you? He's in for a surprise. He thinks he can make a cab driver out of you? Just wait!

Even before the exam, which takes place in the chamber of commerce responsible for cab concessions, candidates are courted by prowling would-be employers. There's a shortage of cabbies in the city, so you're accosted by some rather unprepossessing individuals. Some smell of schnapps, others have beards encrusted with remnants of their last meal.

The examiner calls out several surnames. Mirko's is among them, yours isn't. You wish your friend good luck. Twenty minutes later he emerges with a thumbs-up. Behind him the examiner reads out the names of the next candidates. Kolostrum is the only one he can pronounce.

In the examination room you sit down with three Africans who rub their big black hands, nod to you in a friendly manner, and can hardly speak any German. The examiner, a mustached man with owlish glasses and a blank expression, introduces himself as Herr Hawelka. In a loud, deliberate voice, as if addressing the deaf, he says:

"Since you all hold driving licences, I'll spare you any technical questions. I'll simply test your knowledge of the city layout. Got that?"

The black men nod. You say yes. The examiner asks the first African the location of a street. He answers promptly and correctly. The second man does likewise. You're the third in line.

"Where is Heigertplatz?"

"Sorry, no idea."

He frowns and asks the third African. He knows where Heigertplatz is. So do you, of course, because you live quite near, but this is your revenge on Mirko. You simply won't answer any questions.

One of the Africans, who is seated on your left, whispers, "Geyerstrasse and Waggerlallee" to you but is reprimanded by Herr Hawelka.

"Herr Kolostrum, how long have you lived here?"

"Ever since I was born."

"And this is the best you can do? I can hardly believe that."

"Well, you know, I very seldom go out…"

He brushes this aside with an imperious gesture and turns to the third African, who is excellently prepared like the others and fails on only one street in the course of the exam.

After a quarter of an hour Herr Hawelka signs the examination papers, one after another. Then he reads out the results.

"Herr Bamadou: failed. Herr Diddibum—something like that: failed. Herr Owolowu: failed. Herr Kolostrum: passed."

The Africans get to their feet, looking disappointed, but don't venture to protest. You're so surprised you remain seated, staring at the examiner. Behind you, you briefly hear footsteps and plaintive voices in the passage outside. Then the door closes.

"Why…"

That's all you can get out.

"The local economy needs taxi drivers."

"So why didn't they pass?"

Herr Hawelka sticks his ballpoint in the breast pocket of his blue bus driver's shirt and looks at you expressionlessly.

"The local economy needs *taxi drivers*."

Outside the door, Mirko congratulates you with a triumphant grin and introduces a short, stout individual. He's our new boss, says Mirko. We're going to work for him—it's all arranged. We get 40 percent of the gross and arrange our own shifts, beginning next week.

He says more, but you aren't listening.

NOTE TO SELF: You're staggered to learn that your new boss's first name is Hans-Peter.

On the following day the doorbell rings. Hans-Peter has appeared unannounced. You're to undergo some training, he says. It's the ideal time.

Disconcerted, you get dressed. It's true you need money, but working as a cabby? Out of the question! On the other hand, Hans-Peter doesn't look like someone open to argument. He waits in the doorway and refuses a drink. Come on, he says, no time to waste. He waves a bunch of keys at you. His breath smells of brandy.

Your training consists of Hans-Peter explaining the use of the taximeter, demonstrating the credit card machine, and taking you for a drive. In that brief time you learn that he punishes dissent and slow-wittedness with harsh words. You feel more and more uneasy about him from minute to minute. Mirko told you he had a police record, but he didn't say what for.

"You're a student, aren't you?" he says.

You nod. "Art history."

"Total crap."

That's all he says, so you don't gather whether he means your specialty or university life in general.

He pulls up outside an inn named the Eisenhorn and exits the taxi in jubilant mood. You realized something during the drive. He shot several red lights and his speech is slurred.

The barroom smells of schnapps and stale fat. Hans-Peter says hello all around. Everyone seems to know him. He orders two beers and two schnapps. You're tempted to restrain the barmaid until you see Hans-Peter's expression. His tattooed forearms. His gold chain.

You dig your nails into your palms beneath the table and stare at the dirty tablecloth with your head down. You're startled when Hans-Peter utters an unexpected yell.

"Fredl, you old scoundrel, come and join us! Shut up and sit down!"

NOTE TO SELF: All you want to do when introduced to Fredl is die.

Fredl is also a cabby, you learn. Discounting the barmaid, they're all cabbies in the Eisenhorn, and cabbies are buddies. You have to clink glasses with Hans-Peter and Fredl.

"Everything okay?" Hans-Peter asks thickly an hour later. "Having a good time?"

You nod. You're still too chicken to leave.

"Your first shift's Sunday. Good day for a beginner. Less traffic."

You nod.

When Mirko's cooking dinner on Saturday night and you have to drive a cab the next day, you don't invite Boban for one thing and, for another, find it a drag not to be able to drink as much as the others.

Besides, you're scared. You don't want to drive a cab. You might get mugged. You feel tempted to call in sick, but Mirko would be there and could see when you aren't. What's more, Hans-Peter doesn't look as if he'd tolerate a casual attitude toward work.

On your first day at work you're amazed at how intimidating it feels to drive a Mercedes taxi through the city.

As soon as Hans-Peter is out of sight you park the cab on a side street. Your heart is hammering. You're sweating. You've got a headache. You take deep breaths. What if you had an accident? Would you have to pay for the damage yourself? Everything's so big! Every passerby is a potential fare, a potential threat!

You can't decide whether to drive to a cabstand. You turn on the radio. Nothing but Sunday programs across the dial. You run your fingers through your hair, polish your glasses, loosen your belt, turn off the radio again. You consider driving home and weeping or taking a nap.

Unexpectedly, a man jumps into the cab and calls out an address. You mechanically turn on the ignition. Your hands are shaking. What was name of that street again?

You have a blackout. Right now you wouldn't even be able to find your way home.

"I'm sorry, it's my first day on the job. Where did you say?"

He laughs, sighs, and repeats the address.

The trip takes two minutes, it's that close. You change gear three times on the way. The fare is thirty-seven schillings, he gives you forty. Perspiring and exhausted, you join a cabstand with four cabs waiting ahead of you.

You do some mental arithmetic. Hans-Peter gets 60 percent of the thirty-seven schillings. That leaves you just short of fifteen plus three schillings tip. Not even the price of an espresso.

When you've earned an espresso in an hour you start to bemoan your fate. Especially since your friends are meanwhile sleeping off last night's hangover.

By ten a.m. you've grossed four hundred schillings. By midday, six hundred fifty. By two p.m., nine hundred twenty. By four p.m., still nine hundred twenty.

It's soul-destroying, hanging around for two hours at a cabstand at night. Even if you do have Karl May's *Treasure of Silver Lake* with you.

Your shift ends at five a.m. In fourteen hours you've taken a thousand schillings—in other words, earned four hundred plus tips. The day-shift cabby who drives you home assures you things will get better. You have to learn the ropes. Besides, business is always slack in June.

There are stacks of dirty crockery in the kitchen. The oven window is spattered with melted cheese, the floor littered with fragments of china from a smashed plate. Walter must have felt hungry in the night. You make yourself some breakfast all the same. Shoving bits of melon rind and ham aside, you spread out yesterday's newspaper on the sticky tabletop.

When you sit in the kitchen at five thirty a.m., after your first night shift, you don't—for some unaccountable reason—feel tired. You butter yourself some bread, sip coffee, and read the sports pages. Walter's snores drift in through the half-open door. He never sleeps with his door shut. Birds are twittering outside the window. It's so light, you lower the blinds a little. Everything is so curiously bright.

Feeling relatively chipper, you stroll around the apartment. You clean your teeth. Listen outside Inge's door. Not a sound. Walter, too, has stopped snoring. You return to the kitchen and take a swig of coffee. It tastes bitter after the toothpaste. You catch a fly to prove how fit you are and release it out the window. You leave the window open—the kitchen stinks of garbage—and retire to your own room.

You ought not look at Laura's photo. If you do, you feel a pang in the gut and can't help wondering what she's doing at this moment. Sleeping, you presume, but not—you sincerely hope—with Boban.

Absently opening various drawers and closet doors, you come across the black hat. You shake your head at the thought of how long you went around looking like a village idiot. But now—now you're earning money of your own and wearing an idiotic hat no longer. You're a cabby.

At six a.m. you draw the curtains, get into bed, and fall asleep at once.

At nine a.m. the next-door neighbor turns on his electric drill.

Inge is far from unattractive. You have to know her for a while to discover her charms. She has sharp features and, although she's thin, a pneumatic figure. Her nose is too long, her hair usually greasy, and her feet and hands are so huge you can't help imagining what physical assets she would display, according to her theory, if she were a man. She's no beauty, but there are situations in which you credit almost any woman with an erotic aura.

This realization hits you at six a.m. after your fourth day at work as a cabby. If Inge comes into the kitchen, half-asleep and almost naked, to pour herself a glass of mineral water, you can assume with a probability verging on certainty that you'll experience certain male stirrings. Provided you're a cabby and drive a good-looking woman at least once a day.

When you've been driving a cab for several nights in succession, you begin to regret seeing the sun so seldom. Unless you're roused by a do-it-yourselfing neighbor, you sleep till half past two. Semiconscious, you eat a second breakfast. Shortly before five you're picked up by the day-shift driver. Then you see the sun. By nine it's dark. Then you drive through the night. There isn't much light at five a.m. and at six you go to bed.

"I can't make it tomorrow."

"But you must."

"I don't have the time."

Hans-Peter sighs. In the background you can hear voices and the clink of glasses.

"Charlie, I'm short of drivers. That scumbag Ahmed has let me down again, and his friend hasn't shown his face for a long time."

"I can't possibly."

"But you're my best driver," Hans-Peter purrs. "Nobody got the hang of it as quick as you did. You beat the rest hands down. Don't leave me in the lurch!"

"I really can't."

"Now listen! Who paid for your course and gave you money afterward? Me! Who gave you an advance on day two? Me, you toad! And now you've got no time for me?"

"Okay, I'll do it."

Silence at the other end of the line. Hans-Peter is obviously taking a pull at his glass.

"Shall I come by and put you in the cab?"

"I'll do it."

Another silence.

"Shall I come by and put you in the cab?"

"No need. I'm sorry."

Gurgling noises.

"Be at the Eisenhorn at five."

"I'm on my way, Hans-Peter."

NOTE TO SELF: Silence can be extremely menacing.

Being unable to resist Hans-Peter's pressure—unlike Mirko, who drives when he pleases—you're transformed into a full-time cabby within weeks. Outwardly you pretend it's your own decision. You need the money, you say, and you enjoy the work.

Laura is delighted by the enthusiasm with which you throw yourself into your new job. It was high time, she says. A man must take responsibility for himself. And besides, there's the financial aspect.

"Do you think it's bad, me dropping out of college?" you ask her.

She shrugs.

"Honey, you need to work like everyone else."

Reluctantly, you have to agree with her because you really don't look back on your former plans with any great regret. Art history, bah! Museum director? Absurd. Dreams of working in or with a band? Just dreams. You shouldn't dwell on them too much, though you do admire your voice and style. Time will tell, but you're worried about the future of your relationship.

You work for twelve to fourteen hours five times a week. When do you get to see the others? This detachment from them presents no problem at the moment. It's a new job, and you've plenty of new impressions to digest.

Having come to this conclusion, you wonder how other people in full-time employment deal with the problem. Doing a daily job harbors the risk of ruining any relationship, and the fact that humankind hasn't become extinct since the days of the industrial revolution is eloquent testimony to the human capacity for self-deception, even in the sack.

Come the night when you feel you're in command of the cab and the situation at last, you look in on Mom. Casually, you deposit the car key with the foxtail tag on the table. She goes on stirring her coffee and watching the news on television. You have to wait for the commercial break. She fails to notice the key, so you have to broach the subject yourself.

"High time too. I can't spare you any more cash, not with my overdraft—I was going to tell you anyway. Thank goodness you're earning too now. That's a great relief, Charlie..."

When you're parked at a lonely cabstand, still bemused by this conversation and desperately trying to find an acceptable radio station, your thoughts turn to Aunt Ernestine. You're suddenly overcome by boundless self-pity. At the same time, you're still scared of her ghost and that of the Bonesetter. You think you glimpse something in the rearview mirror. The place is getting on your nerves. With tears in your eyes, you zoom off to the Priamus.

If you're unhappy having to work as a cabby, you should regard it as due punishment for your part in Aunt Ernestine's death.

After two weeks in the cab you have to bring yourself to bid farewell to your love of vinyl and buy some CDs because the cab's cassette player doesn't work, and doing a whole shift without music is almost unendurable. You can't listen to the radio the whole time. You enjoy the nightly two-hour program *Music Box*, but all Austrian radio has to offer aside from that is bestial pop. Background noise of that kind makes you manic-depressive in the long run, so you have to buy some CDs for the cab.

You wince when you hear how much you have to pay for your car-phone calls in the first two weeks. You wanted to stay in touch with Laura, though, and because you can't take a three-hour break every day, you pick up the phone. But why doesn't *she* ever call *you*?

"Why do you never call?"

"I don't want to disturb you at work."

When you wonder if your girlfriend is cheating on you, there are several ways of dealing with the situation. If you want to find out, you will. No need to rummage in coat pockets, check phone numbers, or engage a private eye. Simply asking her will suffice. But you mustn't neglect to assure her in advance of your forgiveness and understanding, tell her that confession is balm for the soul, and say it doesn't really matter anyway. Once you've worked on her for long enough and poured several glasses of wine down her throat for safety's sake, she'll come clean.

After that, of course, there's no further question of forgiveness and understanding. Glasses go flying and doors slam. In extreme circumstances the couple will actually come to blows, a situation more likely to culminate in a visit to the ER than a passionate reconciliation in the bedroom.

Something of this kind can attain such proportions that you can't remember afterward whether it all really happened.

NOTE TO SELF: If you regard enlightenment as something that doesn't necessarily make life easier, you should voluntarily dispense with the knowledge of just how faithful your beloved is.

Saturday is sacred. You don't work a shift on Saturday. Saturday night belongs to Mirko and your friends and Dieter Moor. By now you're experienced enough to allow yourself a bottle of wine on Saturday. You don't have to climb into your cab until four or five on Sunday afternoon. You aren't an astronaut, after all. You can afford to indulge yourself.

One Saturday you catch sight of a scarred face among Walter's friends. It takes your breath away, and your heart leaps. When introduced you stammer and utter some stupid wisecrack. Although Conny has also gone red, you quickly retreat to the stove. A spell has been cast over the room, you notice. This kitchen is the center of the universe.

When you're in a relationship and you suddenly realize you're in love with someone else, you're so stunned you stir around four pounds of TNT into Mirko's oriental stew instead of a pinch of oregano. You're demoted to dishwasher and have to relinquish your obscene apron to Walter.

"I didn't know you and Walter knew each other," you say to Conny.

"But I knew I'd see you here."

She blushes again. Discounting the telling of vulgar jokes, this is the first time you've made a woman blush. You gulp.

NOTE TO SELF: When you know she's interested and she knows you are too, and you know she knows you know, and she knows you know she knows, you both lower your gaze.

Before Laura can smell a rat you move away and engage in an attempt—difficult at this particular moment—to uncork a bottle. You breathe easier when one of Walter's socialist friends engages Conny in conversation, but you still feel a pang.

If you think Laura hasn't smelled a rat, you're making one of the biggest mistakes imaginable: you're underestimating a woman's powers of observation.

After the meal you sit there listening to one conversation or another. Laura is discussing the correct way to make a vegetable chili with Mirko. She's behaving as if they're the only people in the room. If she catches your eye she smiles and winks at you, a form of behavior you find mystifying. Inge and Walter are discussing the significance of her new boyfriend's massive forehead. She has a theory you aren't interested in. Leo and Hilde have withdrawn into a corner with one of Walter's friends. You wonder what they're up to.

"Why have we never bumped into each other again?" Conny asks in a low voice.

"I've wondered about that more than once tonight."

"What's the matter with your girlfriend?"

"That's another thing I've wondered about more than once tonight."

Your tone is sharper than you intended. You've downed a few glasses by now.

When the conversation seems to have petered out, you gaze into Conny's eyes. Rotate the glass in your hand. Blink. Sigh. Feel superheated. You've no idea where this thing is leading, so you feel like someone picnicking with his beloved in a forest inhabited by a prowling sniper.

"How long have you been together?" Conny murmurs, glancing to her left.

"Nearly two years."

"It shows."

Depending on how much you've drunk, wine has a negative and positive capacity for destroying your inhibitions. You've often wondered who you are when drunk: the Charlie who says and thinks and does this or that and weeps over the death of his great-great-aunt, or the one who's rather more restrained and seldom thinks this or that, even more rarely says it, never does it, and least of all weeps in public over the death of a relation.

There's some evidence to suggest that people are their true selves only when drunk. This is a futile realization, however, because it's obvious you can't be drunk from morning to night unless you're a politician, a journalist, or the owner of a cab company.

Wine having destroyed your inhibitions, you question Conny about her private life. You learn that she hasn't had a boyfriend for a year. You raise your eyebrows, exhale deeply, heave a sigh.

What else can you do? Laura is chatting with Mirko, and your head's buzzing. You're drunk.

You've been wondering all the time why Hilde and Leo have been chatting with one of Walter's friends in ever lower voices. Enlightenment dawns when the trio say goodnight and leave together.

"Who were those two?" Walter asks.

"Friends of mine. He owns a leather business, she keeps the books."

"So what are they up to with Ewald?"

You're just about to swallow a mouthful of red wine, and when Walter looks at you like he doesn't know two and two make four, you can't help choking. He slaps you on the back.

When you've recovered you announce you're going to bed. It's eleven o'clock, you say, and your shift starts at lunchtime tomorrow. Mirko and Laura protest, but only halfheartedly. They're in the thick of an argument. Walter raises the strongest objection. Overcome by sentimentality, he wipes the tears from his eyes, burbles something about your having become good friends, and urges you to stay awhile. You shake your head.

Laura says she won't disturb you and will sleep at her place. You give her a nod, momentarily wishing that voodoo or some other form of black magic would make the most frightful things happen to her.

You wave goodnight to the others. Rather than imagine how puerile you must look, you kiss Conny on the cheek.

"But I'll still listen to *Talk Radio*," you whisper to her.

You don't allow her puzzled expression to prevent you from going off to clean your teeth, then striding into your room in a truly lordly manner.

NOTE TO SELF: When you're in a hurry, make a detour.

On discovering that the cat's tray smells like the Black Death, you apologize to Mimi and defer the essential sanitary measures until the next day. A man who has just quit a party with a grand gesture would lose a lot of face if he returned bearing a tray of malodorous cat litter.

Lying in bed, you hear muffled voices issuing from the kitchen. You're far too twitchy to sleep.

At half past eleven you hear someone saying good-bye in the passage. Five minutes later the front door closes again.

At midnight you turn the radio on low and lock the door for safety's sake.

Half past twelve comes, then one. You wonder if you haven't flipped. You ought to get some sleep but you can't. You hear your friends squabbling over the phone outside.

You turn on the light and open *The Treasure of Silver Lake*. Mimi lies down on the book. She purrs even before you stroke her, the minx. You're annoyed you didn't bring anything to drink with you. Laura is still outside. Now and then you hear her laugh.

Dieter Moor gives another caller the heave-ho. The next one is a woman.

"The Café Paradox," she says, "eight o'clock Monday night."

And hangs up.

Dieter sounds extremely puzzled by this information. You put the book away and turn the light out.

However tired you are, you can't go to sleep if you devote yourself to pipe dreams.

You imagine you're in your taxi at a cabstand. A guy gets in with Conny. He has abducted her at gunpoint. You're compelled to drive off. He pulls Conny's hair. You thwart his plans by flooring the gas pedal and speeding through the city like a maniac. Conny and the kidnapper scream with terror. You order him to throw the gun out the window. He hesitates, but he can't afford to shoot you while you're driving so fast. He yells at you. You accelerate still more. You can handle the vehicle at maximum speed, being such a brilliant driver, but the kidnapper gets more and more scared. He hurls the gun out onto the street. You screech to a stop, haul the terrified man out of the car, and twist his arm behind his back. He whimpers. In this position you wait for the cops to arrive. Conny extricates herself from the cab. She gazes at you admiringly and expresses her gratitude. Paoletta, too, has suddenly materialized.

You reprise this fantasy again and again. You tell yourself it's time you went to sleep, but the daydream promptly returns. Dawn is breaking the last time you turn over.

Herr Professor Bennigsen
is the unsavoriest of men.
Scraps of food his beard infest
and there's gravy down his vest.
He's suffering from scrofula.
No wonder he's unpopular.
Herr Professor Bennigsen...

"That's enough," says the woman in the back of the cab. "I've been listening to that for the past ten minutes."

"So sorry," you say, feeling your cheeks burn.

After dropping the woman, you drive to a remote cabstand, put the seat back, and shut your eyes.

A cabby gets plenty of time to think.

The hardest question in any relationship is whether you're still in love with the significant other or simply in love with a habit—with the image of what used to be or the image of what you haven't faded out. Because if you ask yourself whether you're still in love, you fade out everything in the relationship that's discordant. If you're a wimp, at least. According to *Personality*, a wimp is someone who remains in a relationship until the whole thing collapses around him.

When you're an 87 percent wimp you shrink from the thought of leaving Laura and take to the idea of establishing a friendship with Conny uninfluenced by sex.

When you're only a 3 percent adventurer you decide not to show up in the Café Paradox at eight on Monday night and listen to "Cornflake Girl" until you're nearly sick.

Not knowing what to do with yourself after two hours on the outskirts of town, you pick up the car phone and call the Aunticles. You ask how they are. They ask where you are. When you say you're sitting in your cab, Aunt Kathi begs you to be careful not to get shot. A local cabby was recently shot dead by some young hooligan, she says. It could happen to anyone.

You promise to make every effort not to get shot.

Aunt Kathi has been growing odd lately. The fear that her nephew might stop a bullet is only one of the series of strange delusions that have afflicted her for a considerable time. She has banished radio and television from her bedroom for fear their electronics may upset her pacemaker. She also insists that her corpse be stabbed in the heart in case she's buried alive. Naughty Uncle Hans whispers to you that all one need do would be to pinch the batteries from her pacemaker or smuggle a miniature radio into her coffin.

You drum on the steering wheel, spit gum out the window, listen to the news. You can't concentrate, keep thinking of Laura and Conny despite yourself. You feel dissatisfied.

NOTE TO SELF: When you're losing your grip you should do some self-assessment.

But that simple rule is useful only if there's enough there to assess.

It would all be simpler if you lived in an age when heroes still existed. Those days are past, however, so there's no one around to model yourself on. There are times when a wimp who wants his generation to possess some meaning semiseriously debates the truth of the theory that a war wouldn't be a bad thing. War not only cleanses and purifies but presents many a wimp with an opportunity to change his spots—as long as he isn't killed.

You polish your glasses and imagine being in a war with your finger on the trigger of a submachine gun. *Rat-a-tat-a-tat...*

But since there won't be a war and you still can't help thinking of Paoletta, who seems more and more like a character in a movie you saw years ago, you must try to come to terms with the idea that no one will appear who can offer you a lead.

Being grown-up doesn't mean being able to make decisions of your own; it means *having* to make decisions of your own.

When you find you can't see your own genitals unless you're standing in front of a mirror, you should take it as an indication that your consumption of sweet things must be drastically reduced. You seriously mean to do this, but good resolutions get you nowhere on their own. In any case, one of your resolutions was not to approach Conny with erotic intent.

It's an interesting fact that many men attempt to develop friendships with women in which sex is meant to play no part. According to *A Psychological Study of the History of Rock Music*, all such endeavors are doomed to fail from the outset because no such relationship can exist. In any friendship between a man and a woman, the man would be quite prepared to let the platonic, pure, harmonious element go hang and climb into bed right away. Being masters at deception and self-deception, however, men pretend to themselves or their girlfriends that they really feel nothing when lying beside them on the sofa at night, watching some movie.

You know about these things by now, so you suspect that the idea of establishing a platonic friendship with Conny won't be blessed with a successful outcome. So…do you go, or don't you?

Of course you go. You go to the Café Paradox on Monday and Baby Jane's on Friday and back to Baby Jane's the following Tuesday because you both enjoyed yourselves so much. You're in love. You have to go, even though you don't know what to do. Saturday night's dinner is a dreary affair without Conny. You've no appetite. You keep imagining what she's doing. You couldn't invite her, after all.

When Conny goes off to spend a few days with her parents, you drive around town in an even more restless frame of mind. Driving around has suddenly lost its point because there's no possibility of catching a glimpse of Conny on some street corner. You're disconsolate.

You call Laura. She's meeting up with some friends, she says. She may bring them home later on. You hang up with a feeling of brooding anger. She sounds so casual, so self-possessed. Everything seems to bounce off her.

When you're feeling that way and a drunk throws up in your cab, you aren't exactly happy about it.

You stop at a gas station and proceed to swab the seat. This task takes half an hour. The cab still smells so bad afterward, you can't expect anyone to ride in it. While airing the interior you have a soft drink in the gas station café.

The cab still isn't fit for business after another half hour, so you return to the café cursing your karma and buy a newspaper. A boozy party you noticed earlier disperses and a fifty-something woman comes lurching over to you. She asks if you're for hire. Her breath reeks horribly of wine.

You describe the circumstances that brought you there in the most graphic terms, hoping to banish all thoughts of road travel from her mind. She doubles up with laughter. You feel her hand on your shoulder. Women can be gentle even when completely smashed, you notice—gentle and repulsive at the same time.

NOTE TO SELF: Men can only be one of the two.

She orders herself a glass of Veltliner. Would you mind if she waited until the cab was usable again? You've no choice but to indicate the vacant chair beside you.

"What are you doing for the rest of the day?" she inquires thickly, after you haven't deigned to look at her for several minutes.

"Working."

Another silence broken only by the hiss of the espresso machine.

"Take me home, and you can come upstairs with me right away."

You stare at her. Her eyes are glassy. She can't hold your gaze.

The thing to do when propositioned by a drunken hag is to jump up, slap a bill on the counter, and leave the café. You hear the woman call something after you, then you get in the cab and drive off.

You now feel obliged to call Erika, one of Hans-Peter's night drivers. You ask her to look in at the gas station and drive the drunk home. The woman could end up anywhere in her condition, and although you felt disgusted by her you'd sooner spare her certain things.

When you replace the receiver and see that someone has called you at last, all you hear is an electronic answering machine. Because it was Conny, who naturally didn't leave a number, you thump the steering wheel in disappointment. You drive to a drive-in and buy yourself two cheeseburgers and one Big Mac.

Later, Laura calls to say she's staying on for a while, no need to pick her up. In the background you hear noise, music, laughter. You park at a deserted cabstand and turn off the radio. It's pitch-dark. The occasional car drives past. You lower the window. The strains of a dance band can be heard in the distance.

When you've worked as a cabby for a while, it dawns on you that Red Walter is a schnorrer. He never approached you for a little loan before, when you weren't earning. Now he sits on his bed every week looking hangdog and mumbling something about a five-hundred-schilling bill. It's an emergency, he says, and you'll soon get the money back. He omits to say where he'll get it from. You haven't seen him do a day's work since the computer has been in his room.

You give him his five-hundred-schilling bill.

Sitting in your cab when the moon is full, you aren't surprised when it's boarded by an old lady who has forgotten where she lives. She's so confused, she doesn't even notice she's traveling with a little boy, probably her grandson. He slithers onto the back seat first and she promptly sits on him. You have to extricate the youngster. He seems accustomed to such treatment because he doesn't complain. The old lady thinks a passing streetcar is a train but the boy talks her out of it. She also thinks she's in Poland. Taking her shoes off, she orders a coffee.

You make an effort. You talk to her, think up innumerable ways of discovering her address. At last the little boy mentions his father's name. The cab company telephonist looks up his phone number. You call him and he tells you the address. You drive your passengers there and wait for him to collect them from the cab. The old lady turns and calls over her shoulder:

"You ought to leave your wife, Herr Panenka."

If a confused old woman turns and gives you some good advice, it doesn't mean much in itself. But if you're superstitious enough, when shopping in a vegetable market, to devise the most elaborate strategic plans in order to avoid some gypsy beggar woman who might put a curse on you, you don't take such an injunction lightly. Even though you've never gone to the altar with Laura and the name on your identity card isn't Panenka.

Days become weeks. Should you leave Laura?

The disputes over Aunt Ernestine's will are coming to a head. Certain family members have managed to fall out over this question to such an extent that their lawyers and the courts are busying themselves, not with the provisions of the will, but with charges of insulting behavior and worse. During a visit to the Aunticles you lay hands on some details of these cases. They involve name calling, legacy hunting, and demanding money with threats.

All these altercations, all this hatred, all these feuds! They don't appeal to an 82 percent conformist like you, who aspires to peace and harmony. That's why you stick with Laura and sever contact with Conny.

Saturdays are no longer sacred now that you aren't being given any money, even by the Aunticles, because you're earning some yourself. Your cooking lessons in the shared apartment are a thing of the past. Your friends disappear and go their separate ways.

As a cabby you get plenty of time to read. Even on a good day, not more than four out of twelve hours sitting in a cab are genuine working time, in other words, time spent transporting people or things. Because you don't carry human cargo alone. Sometimes your trunk contains a package, sometimes a bicycle or half a pig, and sometimes you're called on to transport human kidneys from A to B, A being usually ten yards from a wrecked motorbike and B a hospital. On one occasion you had to take a guy to the hospital in installments. His liver was ready by the time you'd delivered his kidneys, and his heart necessitated a third trip.

For eight hours a day you can read whatever you like. Even though you don't devote the whole of that time to reading, you extend your horizons and form opinions. You think, brood, ponder on what matters in life. It's not surprising that cabbies are among the best-educated of mortals. You read, mark, learn, and develop your mind.

NOTE TO SELF: When you read a lot, you're surprised at what you used to consider bullshit.

People hail a cab more often in December. The papers are forecasting the winter of the century. Waiting pedestrians often greet you with cries of joy. You're so experienced by now, you know exactly when to park at which cabstand. Or when to take a break because there's a lull in prospect. Or where to eat or fortify yourself with a coffee, maybe with Mirko when he's on the same shift.

Christmas is an exceptional time. Many people claim it's to do with the winter solstice. If you work on December 22 and 23 you encounter an incredibly large number of men and women in tears. The whole city goes hysterical. You're obliged to listen to all kinds of confidences. It defies belief how many wives cheat on their husbands and vice versa, but you wonder why such subjects have to be aired in a cab.

A farmer with protruding ears spends the whole trip sobbing, "Lucy, Lucy, how could you treat me this way!"

Hearing something like that, you wonder if people see themselves as characters in a soap opera.

A businessman wails, "I'm a worm, a piece of shit! Why did I sell Gerda's horse?" The Spanish or Argentinian woman sitting beside him stuffs her hand between his legs and shouts, *"Cojones! Cojones!"*

Or a mother and daughter, age seventy and fifty respectively. The mother: "It's time you started shaving." The daughter: "You went behind Herr Pflegerl's back." The mother: "You might shave off that beard of yours, you look a fright." The daughter (yelling): "You're always so mean to me." The mother: "There are remedies for it." The daughter (weeping): "Herr Pflegerl and Josef know everything!"

NOTE TO SELF: When you're parked outside the central cemetery at one a.m. on the Saturday before Christmas, you start brooding.

Relativizing time is an old folks' habit, they say, but you can't help wondering if it's only two years since ten or a dozen of you held *Twin Peaks* parties. Or if you left school only five years ago.

In a mood like that you ought to try to have a word with Dieter Moor, at least if it's Saturday. You key the number into the car phone. If you're in luck you'll hear a voice telling you to wait.

You light a cigarette although you're driving a nonsmoker's cab for once. The day-shift driver didn't know how to avoid the slippery streetcar tracks and drove into the front of a bank.

It's the first time you've gotten through. The very first. It's important to you to speak with Dieter Moor, and you hope you'll be a match for him. You wait, consumed with excitement. You wait and wait and wait. People get into the cab from time to time. You say you're hired.

"It's only three streets away, you'll be back in no time."

"Sorry, I'm hired."

An old woman comes up. It's started to rain and she's soaked.

"Thank God! Please take me to—"

"Sorry, I'm hired."

"But it's only over there."

When you're desperate for fares as a cabby, nobody comes along. When you're just about to speak with Dieter Moor, you're swamped by them. You remain adamant, however, and call the woman another cab by radio, meantime letting her sit in the back. She gets out with a peevish thank-you when it turns up. You wave your cigarette at her.

A voice says you'll soon be through. You throw the butt out into the rain and nervously feel in your pockets for the pack. You intend to discuss movies with Dieter Moor and interpolate some stuff about personal relationships and self-knowledge.

A tap on the window. You wave the man away. He promptly opens the door.

"Wagnerstrasse."

"Can't you see I'm hired?"

"No, I can't! Okay, let's go."

"I'm sorry, no dice."

In the rearview mirror you see the man making himself comfortable on the seat. He lights a cigarette.

"*Avanti*," he growls.

NOTE TO SELF: *When you hang up without a word and drive off, you know you'll never get to speak with Dieter Moor.*

Although Laura abhors traditions of all kinds because she thinks they're symptomatic of a lack of independence, she has no objection to accepting Arnold and Heike's invitation to a Christmas fish dinner.

"But the Aunticles are expecting me," you complain.

"Don't be difficult, Charlie."

"They'll be sad if I don't show up."

"Arnold and Heike will also be sad if you don't show up, not to mention me."

It's on the tip of your tongue to point out that, in view of Arnold and Heike's cannabis consumption, they'd be as unlikely to spot the absence of an invited guest as they would be to notice if they were sharing the meal with someone they'd never seen in their lives. But you know perfectly well that quips of this kind are better left unsaid. Laura doesn't appreciate them.

By deploying all your charm you manage to get the fish dinner set for eight o'clock. Present giving at the Aunticles will be over by then, and it won't cause a scandal if you absent yourself a little earlier than usual. Arnold and Heike say they've no objection and Laura—with a "For heaven's sake!"—eventually acquiesces.

NOTE TO SELF: If your aunt presents you with a pink terry-towel nightgown for Christmas and explains that it's in case you have to go to the hospital for an operation, you pray that insanity isn't hereditary.

When you've been to the Auncticles' for a gathering at which excessive justice was done to a whole range of Christmas carols, setting foot in Arnold and Heike's bug-ridden apartment doesn't bother you as much. The couple recently got married according to the ancient Tartessian rite, and hanging up all over the place are intimidating objects they describe as ornaments.

After you've done your hosts the honor of taking a few little drags at their joint, dinner is served. It consists of carp with parsley potatoes. You eye your plate suspiciously. Having seen Arnold cook a couple of times, you'd sooner not touch anything prepared by him.

Arnold and Heike eat like animals, and not only in terms of quantity and speed. For a while you watch with secret amusement as Heike wrestles with an unmanageable fish knife, but she ruins your enjoyment by discarding her cutlery and eating with her fingers. You glance at Laura, but she acts like she hasn't noticed.

Arnold jumps up, chewing hard with his mouth open, and goes to the stereo rig to put on some of his beloved reggae. You're thankful to hear Bob Marley's voice because it drowns Arnold's lip smacking.

Conversation revolves around Christmas and Christmas gifts. You tell the story of your nightgown for the hospital, almost yelling because the music's so loud. Everyone thinks it was a charming idea and says Aunt Kathi must be a caring person.

Your hosts soon get around to their favorite topic, documenting the effect of cannabis. Halfway through dinner Heike goes and fetches pencils and paper for you. Because the music is blaring and Heike has monopolized your attention, you don't know how long Laura has been banging on the table and fighting for breath.

NOTE TO SELF: When you see your girlfriend struggling with a carp bone stuck in her throat, it's detrimental to a swift and, more importantly, effective reaction if all present have been smoking grass.

"Tracheotomy!" yells Heike. "She's turning blue!"

She thrusts a fish knife into your hand. Horrified, she paces the apartment swearing to herself. Arnold, standing at the window, wails a descant:

"Shit! Shit!"

You can't count on the others present, and so, despite your pathetic lack of medical knowledge, you have to attempt a tracheotomy with a fish knife. The situation is considerably exacerbated if you don't know where the trachea is.

Prodding Laura's throat with a fish knife, you quickly discover that it's too blunt for the purpose.

"A sharper knife!" you yell. "With a point!"

Heike starts rummaging around in the tool closet. Arnold, still standing paralyzed at the window, mutters unintelligibly. Laura is writhing and gasping. Bob Marley launches into "No Woman, No Cry."

In extreme situations people often react in ways they can't account for after the event. Only shock can explain why you go to the sink, turn on the faucet, and swiftly proceed to sharpen an enormous carving knife.

"What are you doing?" Heike shouts. "Are you mad?"

When you turn around, Arnold utters a scream at the sight of the knife. It's a frightful, bloodcurdling falsetto that pierces you to the marrow just when you badly need a steady hand.

You still don't know where the trachea is, so you stab Laura's throat at random on the off chance. But are you stabbing deep enough? Should you stab above the Adam's apple or below? And how do you know if you've hit the spot? Do you hear a hiss?

NOTE TO SELF: When there are numerous ways of doing something but only one right one, try them all.

You stab above, you stab below, you stab to the right and left, vertically and horizontally. At some stage Heike materializes with a carpet knife in her hand. You hurl the unwieldy carving knife into a corner and snatch it from her. Arnold screams. You snap off the carpet knife's rusty tip. Panic-stricken, you wonder where else to try. Laura's throat is perforated in countless places and the kitchen floor is awash with blood. Her harsh breathing is rapidly growing fainter.

Appalled by this sight, Arnold flees to the balcony, where he starts squealing like a pig in a slaughterhouse. This prompts Heike to lose her composure and start screaming too. The only aid to concentration you can think of is to sing the lyrics of the song blaring from the speakers. You make a few more incisions with the carpet knife. Laura's throat now resembles a joint of raw beef.

At some point Heike has a good idea: she stops screaming and dials emergency.

NOTE TO SELF: If one hasn't studied medicine, one ought at least to do a first-aid course so as to be able to render assistance in critical situations. For Jehovah's Witnesses this is mandatory.

Because you've already—to public knowledge—inadvertently killed someone for the second time, even Inspector Trautmannsdorf is growing suspicious. You fidget around on a grimy chair in the interview room at police headquarters, thanking your lucky stars that no one even guesses at the circumstances under which Aunt Ernestine departed this life.

The hard-nosed cops toss you some photographic close-ups of Laura's throat.

"Is that how someone looks when you 'come to their aid'?"

"How was I to know where the trachea is?" you wail.

"It certainly isn't here." (The bad cop points three inches to the right of his Adam's apple.) "Or here." (He points three inches to the left of his Adam's apple.) "Or here." (He indicates a spot just beneath his right ear.)

"The knife slipped!" you sob.

"Hear that, Trautmannsdorf? The knife slipped! I guess he soaped her throat first. That wasn't first aid, you asshole. Giving someone first aid doesn't mean slaughtering them! The next time you'll gut someone and tell us his appendix was twinging!"

"We'll see what the autopsy says," Trautmannsdorf cuts in. "You certainly have bad luck, my friend. Remarkably bad luck."

"I know. Heike says it's karma…"

"Are you trying to make monkeys out of us?" yells one of the hard-nosed cops.

NOTE TO SELF: When you're under suspicion of murder, it's best to refrain from any esoteric discussions with your interrogators and be 100 percent cooperative.

After being subjected to a series of further threats, you're at last permitted to telephone. You call Aunt Kathi, who evinces no surprise at what you tell her and promises to send you her lawyer.

Two hours later you've signed a statement and are out on the street. You're still in your bloodstained clothes, so no cabby is prepared to drive you home.

When you look like you've just cut someone's throat, people assume you belong to some fringe group. You're compelled to call Hans-Peter and ask him to send a colleague to pick you up.

"You! You also Hauspeterrr!" cries the Turk as you slump onto the back seat.

A couple days after the disaster you call Mom to tell her about it. She says she already heard the whole story from Aunt Kathi.

"Anyway, I never thought you were suited. She: thin. You: fat. She: highly strung. You: lethargic. She: working class. You: from a good family. She…"

You cut this exposition short. You'd like to tell her how you're feeling, but you don't know how to start. She gets in first. She says she's sorry, but you mustn't beat your brains about it. What happened, happened. It was fate. Then she rings off because her favorite soap, *Rich and Beautiful*, is just starting.

NOTE TO SELF: Calling your mother can leave you feeling no better than before.

A few weeks later the doorbell rings. Laura's mother is standing outside. Horrified, you want to dive for cover, but she, an elderly lady with a fine-featured, handsome face, holds out an envelope.

"This was in Laura's savings book. It's eight thousand schillings. I'm sure she'd have wanted you to have it."

Before you can decline the money or even thank her, she turns around and sets off down the stairs. Shaking your head, you plod back into the kitchen.

As you sit drinking coffee with Conny at the kitchen table, you surreptitiously glance at her bare feet. There's nothing sexier than a girl in jeans without any shoes or stockings on. Conny has the prettiest little feet you ever saw. Dainty, with shapely toes and well-kept nails. They aren't crooked or pudgy. Above all, they aren't flat like Inge's.

Since the district attorney rates Laura's death a less serious mishap than that of the Bonesetter, the outcome is a hearing at which you're represented by Aunt Kathi's lawyer, and the experience you gained as Mom's principal witness for the defense doesn't help. Seated beside you in court are Arnold and Heike, whose comprehension of the legal reason why they're sharing the dock with you is precisely zilch.

All the movies you've seen lead you to expect a weeks-long trial complete with jurors and all the trimmings. Instead, you have occasion to note that Hollywood grossly exaggerates, at least in comparison to the Austrian legal system. The hearing lasts exactly two hours and there's no sign of a jury. Utterly panic-stricken by the situation, you concentrate like mad. You make a highly favorable impression on the female judge, not least because you've taken the family's advice for once: you've combed your hair and squeezed into a smart suit.

NOTE TO SELF: *It's wise to know when enough is enough.*

All those involved are called upon to describe their experiences on the night of Christmas Eve. Heike and Arnold make the tactical error of turning up in court under the influence of their beloved brown Moroccan. They mumble, giggle, stare into space so you can positively *see* their brains ticking over, and prove so unworthy of a public confrontation with syntax and semantics that they incur the judge's wrath and are dismissed from the witness box.

In his summation your defense counsel submits that the autopsy has proved beyond doubt that Laura died of asphyxia. The injuries you inflicted were not lethal, he says, nor was death caused by loss of blood. Three inches long, the fish bone found in Laura's throat was directly and solely responsible for her death.

Hearing such statements from the lips of your defense counsel, you're impressed by his fluent delivery and wonder if you shouldn't become a lawyer yourself, especially since several female members of the public are eyeing the fair-haired young attorney with approval.

You're so nervous during the lunchtime recess before the verdict, you spend the whole time sitting on the toilet with diarrhea. A sweetish aroma drifts across from the cubicle next door. Arnold is loud in his criticisms of the judge. She's an insufferable creature, he says. She ought to smoke a joint occasionally—it'd do her good. Doubled up with the gripes, you refrain from commenting on Arnold's remarks and are glad when he puffs himself to a standstill.

Because the judge is an old friend of Aunt Kathi's—something you discover only weeks later—you're acquitted of all charges. Arnold and Heike, on the other hand, are sentenced to a conditional fine for failing to render assistance because they didn't join in the butchery on Laura.

By the time the hearing is over and you're back on the street, a free man once more, you've promised God a score of times to take more care in the future and send no one else to join him.

In bed at night you wonder if Aunt Ernestine, Laura, and the Bonesetter are conferring together in heaven, and, if so, whether you're their topic of conversation, and, if so, whether they're blessing or cursing you.

You tend to believe that Aunt Ernestine has forgiven her great-nephew, and Laura swallowed the carp bone herself. Where the Bonesetter is concerned, however, you feel sure he's only waiting to pay you back.

NOTE TO SELF: When you're not only superstitious but partly responsible for someone's death, you wake up at night bathed in sweat and peer into the darkness to see if you can see their ghost.

You calm down after a while and lie down beside Conny again, summoning up a dream of life as a famous singer. Conny is also onstage playing bass guitar, but you're the star. Thousands of fans are cheering you on. You spot Laura among them. She's alive, and so, by some miracle, are Aunt Ernestine and the Bonesetter. Paoletta is in the front row. A demented fan vaults onto the stage. A karate kick from you sends him flying into the audience. You prance around singing, stripped to the waist. Universal hysteria breaks out, the rock is so cool…

Conny plaintively tells you to stop kicking her.

Once Conny has gone back to sleep, you remember Countess von Dannewitz's advice. After your last experience, trying the smell test doesn't come easy. On the other hand, 3 percent of an adventurer is sufficient to enable you to sniff the neck of a sleeping woman. Sniffing isn't an overly audacious act.

When you sniff Conny's neck you find you have to revise your harsh verdict on Countess von Dannewitz.

When you're working as a cabby you go through time like Spencer Tracy in *Edison, the Man*. You mark time on the spot again and again, and the years speed by like the pages of a flip book.

The main difference between 1995 and 1994 is that you now listen to Stereolab instead of Element of Crime. You move in with Conny. There's a general election. Politics is like water off a duck's back to you. You stay home and watch the results on television. Hans-Peter says he can pay you only 38 percent of the gross instead of 40. He holds out his schnapps. You clink glasses with him.

The difference between 1996 and 1995 is that the apartment usually resounds to German rock. Hans-Peter reduces your cut to 36 percent.

In 1997 Sophie calls you from Egypt. She wants to come home, but her husband won't let her. You put on some trip-hop.

In 1998 you listen to nothing but Tindersticks. Conny retrains as a programmer. Hans-Peter: 35 percent.

In 1999 there are more elections. You don't vote. Nirvana and the rest of the Seattle grunge scene undergo a renaissance. The Turk stabs Hans-Peter when he tries to pay him a measly

30 percent. You switch to Fredl, who has gone independent and "persuades" you to drive for him. When you turn thirty, sheer old age makes you cringe.

In 2000 you listen to Moby and sing along with him all day long. Your fares are an involuntary audience. So are Conny and Mimi. Sophie escapes from Egypt. Faking a dental emergency of life-threatening importance, she manages by devious means to get home with the help of the Austrian Embassy. She weds Boban once her marriage is dissolved.

In 2001 Mirko completes his medical studies and becomes an intern. Red Walter joins radio station FM4. He often bursts into tears on the air. On the retirement of a parliamentarian caught drunk at the wheel, the FIST chairman becomes a member of the National Assembly. Leo is elected to the chairmanship of a football club. You read in the press that Günther, the crazy deputy team leader, has been sent to prison. Uncle Johann wins two lawsuits against Aunt Hertraud but loses one to Uncle Willi from Augsburg.

In 2002 you listen again to Blumfeld. And to Moby. You wear your hair short, not that many people notice because you like to sport a babushka. You look extremely intellectual, much to Conny's approval. When attending cultural functions you dress like a construction worker in blue dungarees and an exquisitely hideous peaked cap. You're bold enough to boo artistes. The movie intellectuals, Boban excluded, come to dinner. They often speak English. You do the cooking yourself, which is a good thing because you stuff yourself with too much junk food in the cab. This has resulted in your weighing 280 pounds on the scales and renders sex practicable only in the jockey position.

When you discuss Austrian Broadcasting's daily talk show with the movie intellectuals, they all agree that only crazies and idiots are prepared to take part in it as studio guests. You never miss one, though. Sometimes one of your friends jokingly suggests attending a show as a member of the studio audience and, if the opportunity arises, taking part in it. Since most people have the occasional good idea which most people refrain from putting into effect, it remains just an idea.

While shopping downtown you're accosted by a girl. At first you think she's touting for donations the way you did so long ago, but she works for a production company employed by Austrian Broadcasting. She's asking people if they'd like to take part in a casting session.

"I'd rather not," you tell her.

You're thrust into a trailer, where you're presented with a questionnaire asking about your personal particulars and career. One of them asks if you have any special distinguishing characteristics.

You love questionnaires and opinion polls of all kinds. You like it when the phone rings and some nice woman asks who you call on Sundays and whether you've recently booked a vacation through a travel agency. You experience a tingling sensation like the one you get when you have to keep still because someone's drawing you.

Your photograph is taken, and the friendly girl asks for your cell number. You half expect to hear from her.

Back home you tell Conny about your encounter. The movie intellectuals, too, are promptly informed. Laughing, they all speculate how bizarre it would be to appear on a talk show.

A few days later, when you're requested by phone to come to the studio for a casting session, you flop down on the sofa and tap your forehead. However, since Conny finds the idea amusing and wants to see her boyfriend on television, no matter in what capacity, you have to go. To calm your nerves you imbibe some Dutch courage. Then, donning your red babushka and your shades, you get a fellow cabby to drive you there.

Having provided you with alcoholic beverages, nibbles, and an assortment of magazines in order to relax you, the production company staff install you in an armchair. Because a mysterious law prescribes that like attracts like—and not only when it comes to money and misfortune, et cetera—your uneasiness prompts you to drink with abandon. You flick through the magazines without removing your shades.

After a while you're joined by a girl named Nadine, who is also facing her first casting session. She's wearing a short skirt.

Certain stallions, when presented with wonderful mares to cover, refuse to do their duty and won't perform until the mares have first been smeared with dirt. This proves that inferiority complexes aren't confined to the human race. You wouldn't normally dare to test the sexual availability of a girl like Nadine, but you lose your inhibitions when she says she suffers from psoriasis.

Because a cat can't help chasing mice, least of all a cat exhilarated by several glasses of Gumpoldskirchner 1996, you start flirting with Nadine. Even though you're an 87 percent wimp, your experiences as a cabby have taught you to devote the remaining 13 percent to getting along with the opposite sex.

You ask Nadine why she's there, and she confirms your suspicion that the interviewer wants to question her in public about her skin complaint. When she asks why you're there, you slap your stomach and say, ironically, that you've no idea, you can't even hazard a guess. You laugh and Nadine laughs with you.

"Will they ask us to appear on the same program?" she asks.

"That's all settled—they told me beforehand. The subject will be beauty and the beast."

She laughs some more, and you glimpse her white teeth. You're far more excited now—it's as if you're already in front of the camera. You go on flirting for a while. Triggered by some kids who come running through the room in which you're sitting waiting, the conversation turns to children. Nadine says she'd like to have children sometime, but not yet. You take another pull at your glass and say there's a way of finding out if her wish will be fulfilled.

You take hold of her left hand, curl her fingers into a fist, and explain that the number of minute creases between the

base of the little finger and the end of the heart line deter-
mines the number of children a person will have. She'll have
two kids one day.

*NOTE TO SELF: If you want to look good to a woman, give her the
impression that you have some experience of the occult.*

"The heart line?" says Nadine. "You mean you're a fortune-
teller?"

In lieu of a reply you take her left hand and run your fingers gently over the lines in her palm. You're sweating even
more profusely than before and suffering from palpitations.

Even if one isn't well-versed in the art of prophecy, one
ought to seize any opportunity to get close to an attractive
woman, make physical contact with her, and convey the feeling that one knows more about her than she does herself.

If she gives you her phone number, you say, there may be
an opportunity for you to tell her more about her future and
personality another time.

Fueled by a shocking amount of alcohol that you can't handle because you seldom drink these days for professional reasons, you devote the ensuing minutes to telling Nadine about
your childhood, singing her a love song really intended to be
sung by a woman ("He's My Guy"), describing your life as a
cabby, and casting scorn on diets. "I am what I am," you say.

Soon afterward, when you're summoned for casting, you
aren't happy at all. You'd much rather have gone on talking
to Nadine than answer banal questions about your attitude
toward life in front of the camera. You've always erred on the
side of safety in such cases, so you refuse to be coaxed into any

scandalous remarks about politics and society, and the casters dismiss you with an insincere smile.

That evening, when you're sobering up, you feel ashamed. Not just vis-à-vis Conny but mainly because of the act you put on in front of Nadine. Why did you do it? Was that the person you really are? The one who surfaces only when he's drunk? If so, the one who's sober ought to destroy the slip of paper with Nadine's phone number on it.

NOTE TO SELF: As someone who has spent his whole life lusting after unattainable women, you'll never dial Nadine's number.

You're surprised to be invited to take part in the talk show after your fiasco of a casting session. Now that the chips are down, however, you wouldn't dream of going. Unfortunately, Conny gets wind of the invitation. She begs and pleads and sulks, and when you eventually let yourself be persuaded she dashes to the phone to tell all her friends. The theme of the program: Day and night—cabbies tell their story.

On the afternoon of the recording you go to the studio with Conny, Mirko, the movie intellectuals, and several other friends, hoping that the preprogram drinks won't affect any of them sufficiently to cause an incident. Appearing in a talk show is embarrassing enough, but being compromised by tipsy friends is an idea that gives you panic attacks when you're sitting behind the scenes having your face powdered by a makeup artist.

When you take the stage—you're the sixth male guest to appear—you're greeted with applause and inexplicable roars of laughter. You know you're fat, but that doesn't usually provoke outbursts of hilarity from other people. You spot your friends in the second row but wonder why Conny is nowhere to be seen.

The amiable female interviewer embarks on some relaxing chitchat. How long have you been driving a cab? Do you enjoy it? You answer monosyllabically, your heart racing. The countless people, the cameras—all this turns the studio into a torture chamber. You curse that day downtown when you chanced to end up trapped by the girl from the trailer.

You feel particularly uneasy as a talk show guest when the interviewer, with a saccharine smile, says you aren't there to talk about driving a cab because the real subject of the program is: *Surprise-surprise, I'm not the person you think I am!*

When a candid camera sequence of yourself with Nadine is shown on a screen, you experience an instinctive desire to throw yourself out the window. It's a dubious pleasure to see yourself coming onto the girl and hear how amusing the audience finds it to watch your elaborate attempts to impress her, nor does it reassure you when the young cabby sitting beside you whispers that this is nothing; he made even more of an asshole of himself. Seething with delight, the studio audience breaks into spontaneous applause at the point where you try your hand at palmistry.

You can't blame them. A man weighing three hundred pounds feverishly coming on to a slip of a girl must be a sight worth seeing.

NOTE TO SELF: It isn't so amusing when you're the man in question.

When the 87 percent wimp in you has flirted away the 13 percent nonwimp, you let everything flow over you: the interviewer's questions; compliments from one or two members of the audience, who tell you you're cuddlesome and they'd like

to take you home to bed and tuck you in; praise from a gig-
gling grandmother who says you're the sweetest of the bunch
and a really nice young man. You even accept the final ovation and shake "Nadine's" hand when she comes onstage to
receive her well-earned applause.

After the program, total strangers bar your path and try to
buttonhole you. You ignore them and go in search of Conny.
Mirko informs you that she walked out, fuming.

After taking a hit like that, it takes you several weeks to make
up with Conny. Justifiably offended, she demands to know
whether you're cheating on her, whether you have a girlfriend,
whether you don't love her anymore. In the cab you're subjected to hourly checkups by phone.

By the time the program is transmitted, your relationship still isn't back on its old footing but has unmistakably
improved. Conny naturally refuses to watch the show on television. You think this an excellent idea.

When a talk show is about to feature you coming onto a
pretty decoy, the best thing is to take Conny on an excursion
into the countryside, pick wildflowers together, and hope that
your days of humiliation will soon be over.

*NOTE TO SELF: A person who has made a fool of himself on tele-
vision gets a lot of phone calls in the days thereafter.*

The FIST chairman calls to say you were "hot stuff," and he
knows what he's talking about.

Aunt Kathi calls to say she's disappointed you still haven't
brought your new girlfriend to see her.

You call Mom. "You were great!" she tells you.

Inge calls and does nothing but laugh for three whole minutes.

Fritz calls from the Priamus. He says he knows someone who knows someone and you're to get in touch if you need anything.

Team leader Klaus calls to say he saw you on the box.

Three strangers call to offer their services as your manager.

Aunt Kathi calls again. She suggests you drop in today and maybe bring your new girlfriend with you.

Austrian Broadcasting calls to inform you that the sequence in which you lie down on your stomach in front of Nadine is to be repeated on a well-known Thursday evening show. Would you be prepared to attend?

After getting an invitation like that, you're completely mystified when Conny insists you go.

"You must be out of your mind," you can't refrain from saying. "Why spin it out after all that's happened?"

When you comply with Aunt Kathi's summons and turn up at the Auncticles', you're surprised to be introduced to an old friend of the family who has switched professions and has a proposition for you.

"Your story could be a money spinner," says ex-Inspector Trautmannsdorf. "When one thinks of all these snafus of yours...I've quit the police, by the way."

On learning that good cop Trautmannsdorf used to be a colleague of Uncle Johann's, you aren't surprised when he hands you a business card inscribed TRAUTMANNSDORF

& CO., PR CONSULTANTS. You know you'll never need a manager, so you readily promise the Aunticles that you'll employ their friend's services if ever you do.

Austrian Broadcasting bombards you with phone calls for two whole days. You're told that hundreds of viewers have called to inquire after the nice, fat lothario who can read girls' palms. You've simply got to appear, it's a great opportunity. An opportunity for what, you ask, but all you get in response is vague, muttered hints.

You can't make up your mind, so it's Conny who eventually calls Austrian Broadcasting and confirms that the idiot from the afternoon program is ready to appear again. It's also Conny who shepherds you to the studio on the appointed day and makes sure you don't run off.

As gruff and diffident during your second appearance as you were the first time, you're glad when it's all over.

To escape any more fuss of this kind, it's a good time to pay Aunt Ernestine a visit. You talk to her beside the grave. Although you know your hairstyle might have annoyed her, she'd have approved of the automobile you drive five times a week.

A biting wind is blowing when you leave the cemetery, and you have to mop your eyes. You sit down in a café and read a paper, catch sight of a huge picture of yourself in the TV pages, and quickly lay the paper aside. Smitten with diarrhea, you make a dash for the toilets. Afterward you buy some breakfast for Conny. You drive much too fast on the way home.

Two days after the broadcast, on Saturday morning, a record company calls to offer you a contract. When the woman with the honeyed voice asks if you have a manager, you look at the business card on your pin board and, as though hypnotized, read out the phone number below the words TRAUTMANNSDORF & CO, PR CONSULTANTS.

Two weeks later you have to go drinking with Trautmannsdorf and the head of Radio 3. The latter brings some of his editorial staff with him. Trautmannsdorf keeps urging you in a whisper to smile and be friendly.

A week later you go to the studio to record a song you've rehearsed. Conny has made you some intermission sandwiches, but they're polished off by the technicians. You stand in an overheated room for hours and sing until the producer is satisfied.

A few days later you and Trautmannsdorf sit down with the man who heads the celebrity section of Austria's biggest weekly. You find him about as likable as deputy team leader Günther.

NOTE TO SELF: Even an averagely well-developed gift of observation enables one to recognize that the world consists almost entirely of deputy team leaders.

You're made to don your red babushka and pose for several dozen photos. Trautmannsdorf wants you to wear some black plastic earrings as well. You comply.

Then your single comes out and is instantly played nationwide.

On the day *Columbia* burns up over Texas, "DJ Fortune-Teller," i.e., you, makes number one on the hit parade with the song "I Read It in Your Hand." You stuff a copy of the chart in your pocket, run downstairs, jump into a cab, and go to see Mom. The front door is hardly open before she starts jigging around, clicking her fingers, and laughing.

NOTE TO SELF: *When you're hailed as a celeb in the press, you get love and kisses from your mother for the first time in ages.*

[THE END]

ABOUT THE AUTHOR

Thomas Glavinic is considered one of the guiding voices in Austrian literature. Born in 1972, he is the author of several novels, as well as a number of essays and short stories. His work has garnered both critical acclaim and commercial success and has been translated into sixteen languages. *The Camera Killer* was awarded the 2002 Friedrich-Glauser Prize for crime fiction and Glavinic was short-listed for the German Book Prize in 2007. *Pull Yourself Together* was number one on the Austrian bestseller list when it was published there in 2010.

ABOUT THE TRANSLATOR

Originally a classicist whose school diet from age eight included ancient Greek as well as Latin, John Brownjohn won a major scholarship to Oxford, from where he graduated with honors. Thereafter, partly because he hails from a ramified family whose members fought on both sides during World War II, he made the transition to modern languages and a career as a literary translator that has earned him critical acclaim and many British and American awards. In addition to translating the better part of two hundred books, he has produced English versions of many German and French screenplays and cowritten several feature films with Roman Polanski.